THE STORY HUNTERS

Anthology

Volume I

ISBN: 978-0-9942556-6-2

Published by Hunter Writers Centre

Introduction

Introductions make me nervous.

My vision of Hell is a meeting room where Lucifer welcomes condemned souls with, "Before we get started, let's go around the table and have everyone share a little bit about themselves."

That's as bad as damnation gets for me: just that same scenario over and over again for all eternity…

So why, then, am I writing this introduction?

Firstly, because I'm honoured to have been asked. But mostly because of how chuffed I am to be a part of this Hunter Writers Centre anthology, and a founding member of 'The Story Hunters' speculative fiction group.

In October of 2017, a ragtag band of Newcastle-based spec-fic writers gathered for the first time. As biscuits and banter were exchanged, we found common ground in our love for tales of other worlds: be they fantasy, future, alien, or the macabre.

Our little group grew over the course of monthly meetings. New members brought fresh stories to the table (and fresh biscuits). At some point, it was decided we should put together a book. It may have been a passing comment at first, the result of too much sugar and zeal, but the idea stuck—and it wouldn't let go.

Writing prompts were assigned to generate ideas.

A pair of dice.

Laundry left out to dry.

A man with a gun.

Some of us took these literally; others went for a more figurative approach. A few of us didn't use them at all, and that's okay too, because regardless of our respective methods, the writing was written.

The twelve stories in this book fall under the broad banner of speculative fiction yet are as diverse as the authors who penned them. Some will awe you with strange places or fantastic technologies. Others are designed to terrify or question the very fabric of our reality.

So please, grab some biscuits, settle in, and allow us to share a little bit about ourselves.

Michael Tippett
September 9, 2019

Contents

Darkest Before The Dawn

by
Michael Tippett

Laura's breath plumed in the crisp mountain air. She examined the revolver. It was heavier than she had anticipated, the chill of the steel numbing her hand.

"What am I supposed to do with this?"

Brian guided her aim to his torso. "You shoot me here. Centre mass. If that moment comes, you do not hesitate. Pull back the hammer, point, and pull the trigger. Got it?"

Laura frowned and suppressed a shiver. The early morning sun shared little warmth as it rose behind a distant peak. "That's not gonna happen, Dad." She lowered the gun, resisting the urge to drop it. "We don't stand a chance without you—and you know it."

Brian scratched the bristles on his chin. "Dammit, Laura. You're a clever girl. Too clever for your own good sometimes. You'd manage."

"No, I wouldn't. You can hunt. Forage. I'm fifteen, Dad, with zero survival skills. We'd be lucky if we lasted a night against those things..."

Those things. Laura fought off the images crawling into her mind. She bit down on her lip to stop it from trembling.

Brian leaned in and held her shoulders. "Listen to me, you are the smartest person I have ever known. If anyone can see this through, it's you. I will teach you everything I can. That includes being ready for situations like this." His grip tightened. "If they get to me, you need to do whatever it takes to save yourself and the boys. Do you understand?"

Laura winced. "Dad, you're hurting me."

Brian let go. His resolve faltered and Laura glimpsed the fatigue lurking in the creases of her father's face. He had aged so much in the past nine months.

Brian ran a palm over Laura's brow. It took her back to her childhood. The nightly rituals where he tucked her into bed and banished the monsters from her room…

Long before the real ones arrived.

"You'll work it out, kiddo." Brian's voice was soft, certain.

Kiddo. He hadn't called her that in years. Laura smiled. Her cheeks ached and she realised how much tension she had been holding in her face.

A pair of tiny voices called out.

Laura glanced back at the weathered motorhome parked in the roadside rest area. "Sounds like they're awake."

Brian stood straight, working the kinks out of his back. "Then let's get them fed and hit the road. We don't want to be anywhere near here when it gets dark."

*

Dusk settled over the lake. Brian cooked by torchlight under the awning of the motorhome. He flipped the fish on the grill and swung his spatula at the swarm of insects around him.

Laura bathed the boys at the water's edge. The twins, Tom and Alex, stood knee-deep in the lake. They made faces at their sister as she scrubbed them with a soapy rag.

Further along the shore, pelicans nestled amongst the reeds. One of the birds took flight and the twins gazed in wonder as it swooped over the glassy surface of the lake.

"A wonderful bird is the pelican..." Laura poured water over Alex's head, teasing suds from his hair as she sang. "His beak can hold more than his..."

Both boys chimed in. "Belican!"

Laura laughed. She scooped her bucket into the lake and splashed water at the boys. Tom and Alex squealed as they splashed back at her. Despite the ten-year difference, it was obvious the twins adored their older sister.

Brian watched his children in the dying light. The sounds of their play carried across the lake, an offering of hope to a world overrun with nightmares. He marvelled at their resilience. After everything these kids had been through…

Brian slapped the back of his neck. He brought his hand around to find fresh blood on his fingers. A mosquito twitched amongst the splatter. He waited for it to stop squirming, and then rubbed it with a thumb until the only thing left was a black smudge.

*

They ate in silence.

Brian finished his meal and sat with arms folded on the table. Family photographs filled the wall behind him, the fragments of their former lives.

The boys picked at their meal with eager fingers. Laura pouted over her fish. She used a fork to scrape the flesh from the bones, taking small bites and relishing none.

Tom's words broke the silence. "When are we going home?"

It was a question he asked on occasion, and one that Brian never knew how to answer. "This is our home."

"I mean our *real* home." Tom pointed to a photograph of a woman laughing as a small dog licked her face. "With Mummy. And Bear. Wouldn't they be lonely?"

Laura dropped her fork and pushed her plate away. She regarded Tom, her lips pressed tight.

"Mummy's dead," said Alex as he chewed. "The monsters came and they got her and she's dead now."

Tom frowned at his brother. "No, she's not. Laura said if we keep her in our hearts then she would never die, so that means she's alive. Right, Laura?"

Alex shook his head. "Nuh-uh, no, it doesn't."

"Yes, it does!" screamed Tom.

Brian slammed a fist on the table. Laura gasped and the boys flinched as cutlery clattered to the floor. The children watched their father. Alex whimpered and began to sob. Tom joined in.

Brian released a ragged breath, placing both hands flat on the table. He opened his mouth to speak…and then cocked his head to listen.

The crickets outside had stopped chirping. There was a new sound—a rumble so low that it could be felt more than heard—and it was getting louder.

Brian stood and rushed to the rear of the motorhome. He

returned with a rifle, chambering rounds as he peered out the kitchen window. "Stay inside, lock the door."

Laura was on her feet. "What is it?"

Brian didn't give an answer as he charged out the door.

*

The growl of the engine grew close. A possum scampered across the road to the lake, backlit by approaching headlights.

Brian had positioned himself against one of the large river gums edging their camp. A makeshift clothesline stretched between the tree and motorhome. Washing flapped in the gentle night breeze.

Brian poised his rifle.

And he waited.

A rusted ute prowled into camp, tyres crunching on the loose road. Its tray jostled with items: jerry cans, fishing rods, crab pots, tools, tangles of rope, and a mound of clothing.

The engine idled as the vehicle rolled to a stop. The driver's door opened. A man, tanned and sinewy, stepped out. He spat on the ground, eyes darting about as he took cautious steps towards the motorhome.

Brian moved from behind the tree. He slipped between billowing sheets on the line, steadying his aim as he advanced on the intruder. "Back in your vehicle and go."

The man froze. He raised his hands and turned to face Brian. "I'm not armed," he said with a nasal twang. "Name's Simon. I need water. Food if you can spare it."

"There's nothing for you here."

Simon sucked air through the side of his mouth. "Come on, mate. That's a big lake. Freshwater too. Reckon there'd be some decent barra if you knew where to look."

"I'll say it once more, get back in your—"

"Dad?" Laura stood beside the motorhome, torch pointed at the ground. "We can't turn him away."

Brian risked a glance at his daughter. "Laura, inside. Now."

Simon grinned at Laura, showing off a mouth of graying teeth. He gave her a nod before looking back to Brian. "I haven't eaten in three days. I'm down to my last drops of water. You send me away now and it's the same as pullin' that trigger. All I'm looking to do is fill the cans, maybe hook a fish or two. You're welcome to keep that thing pointed at me the whole time if you like. Just let me get what I'm after and I'm gone again." He twitched a smile. "Whaddaya say?"

Brian studied Simon through the scope of his rifle, crosshairs firm between the man's eyes.

"Dad? Please…" Laura was closer now. Her plea lingered in the air.

*

Simon picked the gaps in his teeth with a fishbone. He took a mouthful of bourbon, swilling the liquid around his cheeks before gulping it down. "Holy shee-it, that sure does hits the spot!"

Brian sat on the other side of the fire, hands resting on the rifle across his lap.

"Those are some sweet-ass kids you've got," said Simon.

"That girl of yours is somethin'. Got a generous spirit. You don't see much of that these days."

Brian watched Simon, the reflection of the firelight flickering in his dark eyes. He spotted a faded tattoo on the man's forearm. At first he couldn't make it out, but then he realised it was a pair of dice, both of them showing single black dots. *Snake eyes.*

Simon sniffed and readjusted his weight in the chair. "Not much of a talker, huh? Can't say I blame you. Some stranger comes waltzin' into—"

"How did you survive this long? Alone? Unarmed?" Brian's voice was dead flat.

Laura stepped out of the motorhome, closing the door behind her. "They're finally down. I'd say it was too much excitement for one day." Her expression soured. "It's been a while since we've seen anyone else."

Simon eyed Laura as she sat down next to her father. "I was just thankin' your dad. Got a fresh supply of water, even snagged a few flatties. Not sure how I can repay you."

"You can start by answering my question." Brian leaned forward. "How have you managed to stay alive this long?"

Simon turned his attention to the fire. "I was up in Kempsey."

"Kempsey? Bullshit. That place would be a nest, like everywhere else."

"It is now, wasn't before." Simon sighed, shook his head. "You're gonna think I'm batshit crazy, but there was a man there, some old drunk, who could keep the crawlers away. I mean they would go runnin' scared whenever he got near them. Seen it with my own eyes. The locals called him Frank. We all knew him as Mr. Moses, on account of him being able to clear a path right through those nasty fuckers."

"How is that possible?" said Laura.

Simon shrugged. "Couldn't say. We asked him about it, but he would always tell us we were better off not knowin'. There were some rumours. That he got infected and then managed to purge the bug somehow. They reckon he had a stench about him after that, somethin' only the crawlers could smell. Whatever it was, it sure sent them packin'. Cleared most of the town out. Almost felt like we were livin' normal lives again."

Brian reclined in his chair as he pondered Simon's words. "Cockroaches can attract others when they find a suitable place to nest. There was talk about the crawlers being able to do the same. Is it possible this…Mr. Moses…found a way to do the opposite?"

"Who the fuck knows? Not like we had much time to take stock once those assholes in Geneva punched a hole through our world. Shit went south pretty quick after that."

"So why leave if he could protect you?" said Laura.

Simon picked up a stick and poked the dwindling fire. "Old mate got sick, didn't he? We had no way of knowin' for sure what was wrong with him. There weren't any doctors or nurses amongst us. But I seen cancer eat away at someone before. The drinkin' didn't help either. He went downhill fast. Spiked a fever one night and started rantin' about his wife dyin'. Somethin' about how he used his monsters to beat theirs. Nobody knew what the hell he was talkin' about, but I could tell by the look of him that he was a goner. Decided I didn't want to be around when we lost our human insect repellent, so I left the next day. That was three weeks ago."

Brian rubbed an itch at the back of his neck.

Simon downed the rest of his bourbon. He used his boots to nudge another log on the fire. Embers trailed into the night sky. "And what about you? You've kept a family alive for almost a year now. That ain't no easy feat, so what's your secret?"

A noise shot out from a cluster of trees—the sound of rending wood.

Brian was on his feet, rifle at the ready.

The pelicans became agitated amongst the reeds. They flurried their wings and squawked before easing back down.

Laura and Simon stood next to Brian as they glanced about their surroundings.

"You think it's them?" said Simon.

"They tend to steer clear of water sources, especially something this size." Brian kept his voice low. "And they don't usually stray too far from their nest. Could be a straggler."

Another piece of wood cracked in the darkness. Not as violent this time, but closer, more deliberate.

Brian scanned the trees. "Laura, you know what to do…"

Laura nodded. "Please be careful." She hurried inside the motorhome, latching the door behind her with an audible click.

Simon gaped at Brian. "You're not actually thinkin' about going out there?"

"We have everything we need here. If even one of them has broken off and builds a nest—we lose the lot." Brian unclipped the torch from his belt, holding it out to Simon. "You lead."

Simon hesitated before taking the torch. He tested the weight in his hand. "Not much of a weapon. How 'bout a gun? Those trees could be full of them bastards."

"If that were true, they'd be swarming all over us right now… instead of hunting us." Brian tightened his grip on the rifle. "You handle the light, I'll do the shooting."

*

Simon stumbled over a fallen branch, his boots crunching on dead leaves. He swung the torch about, cutting a wild arc of light through the pitch black around them.

"Keep it steady," whispered Brian, "and keep it down."

Simon scoffed. "This torch ain't much help. I can't see shit."

The pair navigated through the maze of trees until they pushed into a small grove. Moonlight bathed the area in a pale wash. Towards the centre, a rotting tree stump stuck out of the long grass.

"This'll do," said Brian. "Go and put the torch on the stump. Stand it up, if you can. We're gonna try and draw it out…like a moth to flame."

"Yeah, except moths don't rip you into little pieces. And that's if you're lucky." Simon trudged off through the grass.

Brian squatted at the edge of the grove, tracking Simon's silhouette through the scope. His nose caught a whiff of something (was it smoke?) but the wind changed and it was gone.

Simon wedged the upright torch into the diseased heart of the stump. He made his way back to Brian, wheezing as he crouched beside him.

The torch was a beacon at the centre of the grove, its light fanning into the darkness.

Simon snorted and spat over his shoulder. "You ever wonder

why they only eat the kids?" His voice sounded strange, distracted. "They'll turn us grown ups—kill us if the mood takes them. But the children? Man, they love the taste of the little ones…"

Brian spotted movement up the side of a tree. He tensed but then released his breath when he realised it was too small to be anything dangerous.

"Don't make sense," said Simon, picking up where he left off. "I mean, I like veal, don't get me wrong, but who doesn't enjoy a big-ass T-bone from time to time?"

"Stop talking," said Brian.

Simon muttered under his breath.

The wind shifted and Brian caught the smell again.

It *was* smoke. But not wood smoke. It could almost be…

He glanced around, spotting a blue-gray wisp coiling from the base of a nearby tree. His eyes strained to make out the tiny object on the ground.

A cigarette butt. Fresh, still smouldering.

Brian fell to his knees as a blow struck the side of his head. He swivelled to aim the rifle but Simon lunged at him and they wrestled to the ground.

Brian's finger clutched the trigger. The rifle discharged, sending chunks of bark flying from a tree. Simon recoiled from the shot—it was all the leverage Brian needed. He shoved Simon backwards and was about to fire when a flash of movement caught his eye.

The second blow to Brian's head hurt a lot more than the first, but only for a brief moment. After that, he didn't feel much of anything.

*

Brian stirred to screams in the night. His head pounded as he struggled to his feet. It took a moment to find his balance. The torch and rifle were gone, along with Simon and his mystery companion. An engine roared in the distance, followed by shouts and wails.

Brian staggered through the dark. His right eye had glued shut from the blood of his head wound. He glimpsed a shimmer between the trees and realised it was the reflection of the moon off water. He followed the traces of light, emerging next to the lake.

Dust roiled along the stretch of road leaving the camp. Laura hugged Tom on the ground outside the motorhome, both of them crying as they clung to one another.

Brian bellowed—the roar of an animal, primal and fierce—as he hobbled into camp. He grabbed a towel as he passed the clothesline and held it to his head.

"Dad!" Tom scrambled to his feet. He locked his arms around Brian's legs.

Laura stood, tears spilling from her face. The torn collar of her shirt hung off a shoulder. "They took Alex…they took him! I tried…"

Brian pulled Laura into the huddle and held her tight. He spotted the dust settling on the road. "We're leaving. Right now."

"How are we going to get him back?" said Laura, her voice strained with emotion.

Brian broke away and hurried inside the motorhome. Laura and Tom followed.

Their home was ransacked, the contents of drawers and cupboards strewn across the floor. Brian ignored the mess as he ran a hand along the top of the kitchen pantry.

"There's a woman with him," said Laura. "She tricked us, Dad, into opening the door. They said you were dead." She was crying again. "What are we going to do about Alex?"

Brian pulled down a black pouch and removed the revolver inside. He checked the rounds in each of the chambers, locked and spun the cylinder, then turned to face Laura. He could feel the heat radiating from his face as he spoke in a voice edged with steel. *"Whatever it takes."*

*

They found the ute a few kilometres down the road, dumped in the parking lot of a ramshackle motel. Both doors were open and high beams left on, blasting the front of the motel in stark light. Alex was visible in the driver's seat. He thrashed about, fighting with the rope that bound him to the steering wheel.

Brian slowed the motorhome as they neared the entrance. His instinct was to speed straight towards the ute—but he wasn't falling for any more ambushes tonight.

Laura sat beside him, holding Tom on her lap. "They left him there? Why did they do that?"

Brian scanned the rooftops. Dark shapes were gathering. A bolt of adrenaline shot through his body. "It's a nest. They wanted bait…a distraction while they looted."

Laura sucked in a breath as the shadows rippled over the building. "Dad, they're coming!"

"Hold on to something." Brian floored the accelerator. The motorhome jumped the gutter and ploughed down an embankment into the parking lot. It skidded to a stop near the ute.

Shrieks pierced the night as crawlers rained from above. Chitinous bodies with disproportionate limbs and barbed talons scuttled towards the motorhome.

Brian raced for the door. He snatched a carving knife from the kitchen bench before bursting out into the lot.

Alex spotted his father. He yelped and yanked at the rope. "Dad, the monsters!"

"Hold still." Brian slashed at the binds with the knife. The rope frayed, snapping as the first of the crawlers reached them. It pounced on the bonnet of the ute, its once-human face hissing at them amongst thrashing talons.

Brian dropped the knife. He pulled Alex out of the vehicle with one arm, using the other to whip the revolver from his belt. He fired two rounds into the creature. It flailed and fell to the ground.

Brian lifted Alex and dashed for the motorhome. He could hear the swarm behind them—the spitting and clicking of razor-sharp limbs on asphalt. Laura and Tom were standing in the doorway, screaming and waving them in. The chittering of the crawlers was so close that Brian swore he could smell their rancid breath. Something brushed his leg and he almost tumbled.

Brian reached the door and hoisted Alex into Laura's waiting arms. He was about to follow when a creature latched onto his back. He yelled and angled the revolver back over his shoulder, firing three quick rounds. There was an ear-splitting shriek. The crawler released Brian as something forced itself into his mouth. He gagged as it wriggled down into his stomach.

Brian dived into the motorhome, kicking the door shut as a crawler rammed the other side. He jabbed a pair of fingers down his throat, hoping to vomit the thing that was unfurling inside of him.

Laura rushed towards him, the two boys cowering behind her. "We're surrounded!"

Brian buckled as a searing pain shot up his spine and jolted his skull. He dropped the revolver, fingers cramping into claws. The creature inside was fighting for control.

Crawlers bashed at the walls. Talons raked the ceiling as it strained under an increasing weight.

Brian screamed. His back arched to the point where Laura thought it might break.

"Dad, what's wrong?"

"I've got one in me." Brian struggled as his hands seized, the tendons stretched and knuckles pinched white. He smacked the revolver with the back of a hand. It spun as it skidded, stopping at Laura's feet. Brian spoke through clenched teeth. "Laura, you know what you have to do…"

Laura looked down at the gun. She shook her head as hot tears spilled from her eyes. "I can't."

Brian was on all fours now as the darkness burrowed into his brain. He snarled at the children, aware of their enticing scent. "Laura…*please.*"

The roof at the rear of the motorhome collapsed. Crawlers spewed in, thrashing and gnashing towards them.

The twins screamed, hysterical with fright. Laura stood in front, shielding them from the encroaching swarm. She snatched up the gun, trying to steady her shaking hand.

Laura spoke through sobs. "We need you, Daddy."

She watched the last of her father's humanity dim in his eyes. He poised to pounce. The monster inside had beaten him.

He used his monsters to beat theirs.

An image flashed in Laura's mind. A frosty morning in the mountains. Her father running a hand over her brow, the way he used to when he chased her nightmares away.

You'll work it out, kiddo.

Laura blinked as if someone had slapped her in the face.

Her breathing slowed. The shake in her hand subsided. She glanced at Tom and Alex, the love brimming in her eyes. "*They* need you, Daddy."

Laura cocked the hammer, the way her father had shown her, slid the barrel into her mouth…and pulled the trigger.

*

The shot rang out in the narrow confines of the motorhome.

The twins squealed as Laura's body hit the floor.

Brian roared. It was an utterly inhuman sound at first, but then emotion flooded in as his mind reeled at what had transpired. He shuddered and heaved. Vileness rushed up his throat and expelled itself onto the floor, a pool of blackened bile and alien viscera.

The crawlers pouring into the motorhome shrieked and flounced. They trampled each other in their desperation to escape through the hole in the ceiling.

Brian pulled the twins in, hugging them as they wept. He then shuffled to his daughter's body, cradled it in his arms, and started howling as he rocked back and forth.

The first tinges of dawn were bleeding into the sky as they emerged from the motorhome. Brian carried Laura's body. Tom and Alex huddled close, clutching either side of their father's pants as he led them towards the motel.

The boys whimpered at the sight of the swarm covering the building. The crawlers stirred, their twisted shapes sensing something in the air.

In the distance, a rifle fired once, twice, and a third time, followed by strangled screams and then nothing.

Tom and Alex sobbed as they neared the infested motel.

Brian stared into the writhing mass, unblinking, unfaltering. "Don't be afraid," he said. "You don't ever have to be afraid again."

As Brian and the twins approached, the crawlers parted. They then dropped and scattered, fleeing back to whatever nightmare they had escaped from.

Missionary

by
Peter Mark Lewis

The pilot's voice rang inside my headphones.

'We're making a slow south-western approach to one of their larger villages. There's an open square big enough for us to land and that will be our drop-off zone. After we set down, our soldiers will cover you, but only until you establish communication with their headman. Once we're sure the locals aren't going to kill you, we'll take off again.' There was a pause before he added, 'Then you're on your own.'

The intercom went dead before I could respond. The pilot was no more interested in my work than the soldiers who were sharing the cramped cabin with me. I sighed to myself and felt the same old nagging doubts I always felt when taking god to the ungodly. It wasn't easy being a missionary.

My rear end ached. The tiny seat was barely adequate for the task of holding up my ample posterior, but there was no point complaining to the others; most of them were sitting on the floor and would be in no mood to provide sympathy. I turned instead to stare out the window at my new home. It seemed quiet enough from the air, peaceful even.

We were flying below the cloud layer now and moving at a steady throbbing pace over a broad mass of trees. The foliage was lush, like a deep green carpet, and filled with birds of every description. The flocks took to the sky when they heard us approaching, treating me to a display of exotic colour that took my breath away.

The forest rolled onward to the edge of a river; a long serpent of water so clean it could have been made of blue glass. Shoals of fish rippled the mirror of its surface, creating circular patterns that fanned out in ever widening circles.

Looking down on the pristine beauty of this place, I found it hard to believe the advance reports of violence in this remote paradise. Murder was supposed to be a routine occurrence amongst the native population.

I felt a wave of apprehension and turned to the soldiers, my would-be protectors. They were a motley group: tough in the way that veteran fighters always are, with cynical expressions and dull eyes. The vista beyond the windows held no interest for them, and they passed the time preparing their fearsome array of weapons. Only their officer showed signs of an active mind, but he seemed distracted by his intelligence report and was loath to involve himself in conversation.

My attention was returning to the window when a gruff voice interrupted.

'Pretty, ain't it.'

I blinked in surprise, then looked around the cabin. One of the troops, a sturdy individual with small cruel eyes, was regarding me with amusement.

'I beg your pardon?' I replied.

'I said it was pretty,' repeated the soldier. He puffed smoke from the corner of his mouth and watched it rise into an air-conditioning vent. 'But don't be fooled by all that nature shit. Just because they ain't got no fancy technology like us don't mean they any different. Beneath it all these guys are the same as everywhere else. They'll treat you fine until push gets to shove and then BOOM!'

He pretended to fire his weapon, making me jump. Several of the others snickered, enjoying my discomfort.

I sniffed at them. 'It's my experience that there's good in every heart. It's just a matter of bringing it out.'

'Yeah?' replied the soldier, his thin mouth curling. 'Well, you watch these natives don't bring your soft little heart out of your chest and serve it to you on a plate.' He paused to exhale more smoke, then added, 'I seen enough in my life to know what's good and what ain't.'

I opened my mouth to say something, but no sermon came to mind that would convert these brutes to my point of view. Their officer gave them a look that shut them up, but he appeared to be no more sympathetic to my cause than they were, so I turned my attention back to the landscape unrolling beneath us. The forest was giving way to simple dwellings, and boats could be seen venturing out on the river.

'They've never been touched by civilisation,' said the officer. He was staring out the window, but I could tell his words were aimed at me. 'Maybe they'd be better off if we left them that way.'

'Perhaps,' I replied, 'But then they'd never learn the true nature of existence.' I held up the Good Book as if to shield myself from his doubts.

'Yes,' he said, his eyes never leaving the window. 'How could I forget the purpose of this mission.'

I snorted. 'We're here to help them become more than they are. You can't have morals without religion.'

'Strange,' replied the officer, holding up the intelligence report as if in answer to the Gospels. 'This says they have both ethical and religious beliefs, and that they aren't necessarily tied to each other.'

I was beginning to prefer the company of the soldiers over their commander. Rather than answer him straight away, I turned back to the window and looked down on the natives. They were aware of us now and swarming like ants out of their little dwellings as we flew overhead. The village square was visible not far ahead and the pilot was descending toward it at a measured pace to avoid exciting them any further.

I turned my attention back to the officer. 'This mission will bring many positive changes to these humble folk.'

'Yes,' he agreed, 'They'll discover all the benefits of civilisation.'

'Quite so,' I replied, pleased at his affirmation.

'And,' he continued, 'They'll exchange their simple tranquil lives for our complex stressful ones. We'll bring diseases and addictions they've never heard of, and when they get sick or desperate, we'll dangle our sophisticated health systems in front of them while providing very little real help.'

'You see only darkness where I see light.' I replied, my anger rising again. 'I'll help them learn how to create a civil society with a rule of law. Legal systems will bring order to this chaos we see before us.'

'True,' he replied, nodding, 'They'll adopt our multitude of laws to replace their simple ones, and in time they'll march in lockstep with all of our petty social inhibitions, or risk seeing their remaining freedoms disappear behind prison bars.'

I groaned under the leaden weight of his negativity and turned once more to the window. We were close enough to the ground now to see the native's faces, and they appeared to be both amazed and frightened by our airborne presence as they turned and ran for their lives. Damage to their isolated way of life had become irrevocable. It was too late to turn back now.

The village square was bigger than it seemed on the map so there was plenty of room to land once the inhabitants had scattered, and I watched the grass swirl in intricate patterns from our downdraft as we came to rest. The pilot cut the engine, and when it throbbed to a halt we were surrounded by an eerie silence, as if this remote community was holding its collective breath.

The officer interrupted my thoughts yet again. 'They might not know *our* God, but they certainly know *their* gods. They also know wars and violence, but not on the vast scale that we practice them. They have communities, life-long marriages, and they care for their elderly and children, so they certainly know how to love.'

He put down the intelligence report and watched the natives coming back out of their hiding places. Curiosity was replacing their initial wave of fear. He gave me a long hard look.

'Yes, Missionary, they know how to live, they know how to die, and they know how to pray. Perhaps they should be teaching us the nature of existence rather than the other way around.'

A crowd had gathered outside, and it was clear they viewed our arrival with mixed feelings. It was showtime. I shrugged off the officer's depressing philosophy, opened the door and emerged very slowly to avoid alarming the warriors that encircled our landing site. They carried primitive weapons and it was clear they were prepared to use them. My own guards remained hidden from view, but they were ready for anything. Despite their unpleasantness, I was glad they had my back at such a crucial moment.

I took a deep breath, undulated down the starship's ramp until I could feel the grass of New York's Central Park beneath my pedipalps, then held the blessed gospels up with one of my tentacles and announced in the local language, "Take me to your leader!"

Dilemma

by

G. N. Warren

They say words have power.

I don't know who 'they' are, but I believe them.

'Your chip is missing.' My doctor says it again like I didn't hear.

Four simple words, but so powerful. Powerful enough to change my life in an instant.

'Are you sure? Let me see.' I slide off the exam bed and walk around behind him to look at his monitor. But I'm not interested in what's on the monitor.

I bend down and slip my arm around his neck, wedge his throat in the crook of my elbow and squeeze, just like I was taught. I am surprised how easy it is, but then I am a fit man of 35, and Dr Charleton is a thin man in his 60's. His hands claw against my forearm, his gasps a soft wheeze in my ear.

But I can't do it. I'm an accountant, not a murderer. I let go, and he slumps in his chair. A training drill is one thing. Trying to kill someone who I've known for 20 years is another. I touch his neck and check his pulse, maybe detecting a faint push against my fingertips. No time to be sure.

I step out into reception and close Dr Charlton's door with a light click. I force myself to walk, despite every shred of my body screaming at me to run.

The receptionist gives me a bored smile as I pay my bill, 'Will you be needing to make another appointment Mr Allen?' She asks.

'No thank you.' The ball of terror in my throat softens my voice to a rasp.

'You OK?'

I clear my throat. 'Sure,' I say and return her smile. It feels like a grimace.

I walk down the stairs to the foyer and force myself to walk until I reach the park. I sit on an empty bench deep in the shade of a giant fig tree.

I look at my right forearm, wrapped in the soft bandage covering the scald burn I received three hours ago. The reason why I went to Dr Charlton. The man who had supported Emily and me for five years while we tried to have a family. The man I just tried to murder.

How was this possible?

When Dr Charlton scanned my arm, my ID chip should have identified me to the computer. Chips get damaged, which is why Dr Charlton would have checked, but they don't go missing.

I know it was there a month ago because I wouldn't have been able to get through the shuttle port without it.

Two explanations, one impossible. So, someone has removed it. But who?

My employer is one of the most dangerous and unforgiving men in the city – I could have done something to warrant my death. But wouldn't sending one of his men – the ones who taught me how to strangle a man – be simpler?

I hear sirens blare as police and emergency vehicles blast past the park. No time to sit wondering. I get up from the bench and walk in the opposite direction, back towards our apartment. I force myself to continue to amble along, despite feeling every eye in the city on my back.

*

Emily is at the apartment, standing in the kitchen when I get home. 'Why are you home?' I ask.

'Could ask you the same thing.'

'I was at the doctor's.'

'Why?'

'I burned my arm,' I hold my bandaged arm out to her.

She makes no move, unwilling to close the distance that has grown between us in the last few months, 'Doesn't look that bad,' she says.

'Emily… I –'

'You could have gone back to work,' she looks worried now. 'Mr. Zhao won't suffer your absence for long.'

'I know. Emily listen,' I raise my voice a little. 'My chip is missing.'

She looks at me. Stunned. 'What?' Her voice is a whisper. She cries, sweeping her head from side to side and chanting no over and over again.

I walk into the kitchen and hold her shoulders in my palms, 'Emily, please. I –'

'NO,' she shrieks and flings my arms away from her. 'Stay away from me.'

The sudden violence of her reaction shocking me off balance

33

and I stumble backwards.

She's shouting at me now, 'Get out. Go away. Get out. GET OUT!'

Fifteen years of marriage and we've come to this. I can feel her anger. I feel my anger rising but despite the distance that has grown between us, I love her, and I can't refuse her. So I leave, scrubbing away my tears as I stumble down the stairs.

I walk. My mind wanders. Too many impossibilities in one morning to focus. Too many questions I am sure that I won't find answers to before it's too late.

I sit on a low bench, ignoring the people passing in front of me. After some time, my phone buzzes. I tap my implant, 'Hello?' ID BLOCKED flashes before my eye. 'Who is this?'.

'Now's not the time, David,' a man's voice. Familiar, but hard to identify on the lo-fi audio connection.

'What the hell is going on?'

'I can't tell you over the phone. You must meet with me.'

'Where?'

'Low Side. You know where.'

'What?' Several passers-by give me startled glances as I growl into the air, 'How the hell am I supposed to get to Low Side without a ...' I stopped, aware of the many sets of ears around me.

'You'll find a way,' he says. And hangs up.

As the sea rose over the years, the city built a concrete wall to stop seawater inundating the upper city. The seaward side of the wall has been pejoratively called Low Side for at least two generations.

A diverse community inhabits Low Side, common only in their

inability to afford accommodation in the city. Various criminal gangs are the undisputed masters of Low Side, waging bloody warfare with arms more often than not supplied by my employer.

My employer maintains a storage warehouse in one of the few places in Low Side high enough to escape the storm surges. I know this is where the caller wants me to go, but the one official access point between Low Side and the city is also the most fortified and patrolled entry into the city. It would be impossible for me to get to Low Side through there.

But there are other ways to get in.

*

The warehouse sits a few metres from the giant concrete wall separating Low Side from the city. The late afternoon sun throws deep shadows across the base of the wall and the warehouse. I run along the wall, more worried about someone smelling the filth of the sewers on me than seeing me. Halfway along the side of the warehouse is a small door leading into a men's urinal and change room. The door is unlocked.

I walk through the change room and out into the warehouse, my eyes adjusting to the dark. Ahead of me, rows of steel columns stretch out and up into the darkness. A man steps out from behind a column to my right.

It's me.

I can't find any words. I look at him, look at my arm. Look at him again.

Two explanations, one I thought impossible.

I find my voice, 'I'm a clone?'

He nods; sadness in his eyes.

'But why?'

'It's the only way we could get away. To escape Zhao.'

'We?'

Emily steps out from behind him. My Emily. She wraps her arms around him and tries to smile.

'I don't understand.' I say.

'I have been skimming cash from the casino and the brothel for months, He says. 'The only way I could do that without Zhao suspecting me was to keep turning up every day.'

My head is spinning. Too many impossibilities, 'Months you say? But I can't have been without a chip for more than a month. I …'

The truth hits me. He confirms my horror by looking away and then at his feet like a chastened schoolboy. 'How many clones?' I ask.

'You're the fourth.' His voice is a whisper.

'Four clones? Where did you get that sort of money?'

He shrugs a backpack off his shoulders and takes out a thick, leather book. I recognise it immediately – Zhao's ledger book. Every major contract, contact, distributor and client is in that book. 'Zhao's competitors will pay handsomely for this,' he says.

'How could you?'

'It wasn't supposed to work out this way,' he looks up at me, his eyes glistening, pleading. 'If you hadn't burned your arm you would never have known. The others we euthanised in their sleep the night before I had to travel. They knew nothing.'

I feel sick. I wish I could be like the others and know nothing of this. You can load clones with whatever memory set the buyer wanted. I have a lifetime of memories – my childhood, school and graduation. Memories of earning my accounting degree, and my delight at being recruited by one of the city's most successful businessmen. It was only later I would learn that Mr Zhao was also a criminal tyrant to whom disloyalty meant death.

Memories of Emily, of our first date, of our deep and shared love. Of the highs and lows of trying and failing to have a family together. Of the deep love I still hold for her.

But they're all lies. I have no memory of my duplicity. No memory of turning into a thief. Of committing murder in the middle of the night. Of becoming a monster to escape a monster.

I look at him. He says nothing. In the silence, I hear a cacophony of sirens, growing in volume and urgency as they approach.

He reaches into the backpack and pulls out a neat white microchip gun and an ugly black submachine gun.

I understand why he called me here. I shake my head as tears fill my eyes, 'I don't want to die.'

'Please David, you must do this,' Emily steps towards me. 'We have to leave, but if Zhao or the police think we've escaped, there's nowhere safe for us.' She turns and takes the guns from the other David and holds them out to me, 'Please.'

I take the guns, my hands shaking, 'But, I love you.'

'No, he loves me. They're not your memories. If you don't do this, we all die.'

I look at the guns in my hands. I look her in the eyes. I do love her, so I can't refuse her.

I push the microchip gun against my wrist, firing the chip through the bandage and into the skin below. I hand her the microchip gun and take the submachine gun in both hands.

Emily mouths a silent thank you, a single tear sliding down her cheek as she turns away.

I walk towards the front doors of the warehouse. The noise outside has grown to a roar of sirens, helicopters, drones, and demands for my compliance.

My phone buzzes in my skull. A message from Zhao flashes across my vision. *I am disappointed with you,* David.

I click off the safety on the machine gun and pull the bolt back. It's an effective weapon, but no match for the firepower gathered outside. I'm not planning on shooting anyone with it anyway.

Emily won't be disappointed.

I look back into the warehouse. 'I love you,' I call into the darkness. There's no answer.

I turn back to the door, take a deep breath, pull the door bolt, and step out into the dusk.

Batch Eleven

by
Graham Davidson

Sandra moaned once more, louder this time. It was no longer appropriate to ignore her.

I turned from the computer screen and looked at where my mentor lay on a gurney just metres away. Two weeks of working around the clock was taking its toll and she'd now succumbed to the very plague we'd been fighting.

I rubbed the sweat from my brow and whispered, "I'm not up to this."

Again, she moaned. Trails of perspiration poured from Sandra as she strained to lift her head. Her face now bore scattered lesions that had only appeared in the past few hours, and her belly was swelling. Her time was almost up.

I turned my attention back to the vials lined up on the desk, each one labelled from one through to twelve. Time to make a choice. One last chance before the parasites inside her burst free, leaving behind a lifeless shell.

Seeing the anguish writ large on my face, Sandra reached out, attempting to touch my knee. Her voice was a cracked whimper. "It's the only way."

I nodded, then made my way to her desk by the window at the far end of the lab. I opened the drawer that held little more than a deck of cards and a pair of dice.

No research papers or thoughtful analysis, just meaningless tools of chance. How ironic.

Closing my fist on the dice, I found my eyes drawn to the window and its constant reminder of the stark reality facing humanity. They hung from every balcony, eerie in the light of the imminent storm. Individual bloodied pieces of clothing… each one a warning.

Another anguished moan from the other side of the room reminded me of my urgent task.

I rolled the dice.

A flash of lightning highlighted the result, the ensuing roar of thunder adding punctuation.

Eleven.

Packing away the dice, I returned to the mentor who'd become my patient. Heavy rain began hammering against the window as I removed the cap from the vial of Batch Eleven and extracted its scarlet contents into the syringe.

Sandra asked, "What was it?"

"Six and five."

"Urgh! You've got to be joking!" She turned her head away. It was hard to hear her over the thundering of the monsoon-like downpour developing outside. "I've never had much luck with eleven."

"Do you want me to roll again?"

She grimaced in response to the repetitious outward stabs from her belly; once, twice, three times, then some more. I could almost see the swelling incrementally increasing as I watched each flinch of pain. The lower two buttons on her blouse had already popped. Another was just about at its limit. "No," she said, "let's just get this over with."

I pulled the tourniquet tight, making the last viable pockmarked vein in her arm stand up.

As soon as the needle touched her skin, the vein retreated.

I'd heard from nurses about this phenomena, but had never believed them until now. "The vein, it's disappeared."

"Do the ankle."

"Won't that hurt?"

"Hey, I'm in a world of pain anyway." Her fingers felt ice-cold when she reached out and touched my hand. "Just do it."

Having found the vein, I pushed down on the plunger.

Sandra screamed.

Reaching up with my gloved left hand, I tried to cover her mouth and stifle her voice.

She pushed my hand away. "What was that for?" The question had been sandwiched between desperate gasps for air.

"We don't want to draw their attention."

She rolled her eyes then changed the subject. "Make sure you give yourself a shot. We need to stick to protocols."

What?

Like rolling the dice?

Despite my cynicism, I filled a fresh syringe, flinching a bit as I pushed it into my vein, then squeezed down on the plunger.

Sandra looked toward the window. "It'll be dark soon. Time to shut down."

"We need food."

"I don't."

I'd long since given up arguing. Like before, when I came

back with food, she'd more than likely eat a mouthful or two. "There's some muesli bars and chip packets left in the machine downstairs." I got up and walked to the door.

"Have you got the hammer?"

"I won't need it."

"Take it anyway."

I grabbed the claw hammer we'd been keeping by the door and put it down next to her on the gurney. "If they come, you'll need this more than I will." The truth was, I couldn't stomach the idea of having to use it myself.

I put on a surgical mask and opened the door to the corridor.

The mask did little to disguise the stench of rotting remains that littered the wide passageway. Every corpse was the same, like an explosion had come from the belly. But it was more than that. The flesh, even on the newer corpses, was so emaciated that it was like they'd been sucked dry.

I made my way downstairs to the vending machine I'd smashed open a few days earlier. I'd taken what I could carry then, but knew there was more I could come back to.

On reaching the bottom of the stairwell I stopped.

As the door creaked open under my guidance, I knew something was wrong. Muffled sounds came from the corridor.

Someone was out there.

Going against my gut instincts, I stepped into the middle of the corridor and watched the middle-aged man with the swollen belly gorge himself on the remains of the vending machine's contents. He froze when he felt my presence, then slowly turned to face me. The stethoscope hanging from his neck told me he was a doctor.

He looked puzzled. "We haven't got you yet?"

I froze. If he was saying "We" that could only mean one thing.

It was too late for him.

He was ready to pop.

The doctor approached, then paused. He rolled his eyes upward and blood spluttered from his mouth as his belly expanded further, like a balloon connected to an air-compressor. He fell to his knees and stared at the ceiling with arms spread wide and his jaw hanging open.

There was a pregnant pause; a moment of eerie silence.

A loud splat filled the corridor when his belly burst, coating the walls with putrid slivers of something akin to rotten flesh. Despite the surgical mask, my nostrils were assaulted by the pungent stench of sulphur dioxide and ammonia

The worst of the plague then played out before me.

I wanted to run but had to see for myself what others had tried to explain to me.

Every small piece of the flesh-like substance splattered on the floor, wall, and ceiling began moving. They seemed to have lives of their own.

I sat mesmerised for the minute or two it took for them to come together, first as a nondescript pile of organic stuff, but then quickly forming into a naked replication of the human whose broken remains lay on the floor.

A parasitic phantom.

Once fully formed, it casually turned to me and said, "You, your name's Danny." The voice sounded electronic and distorted. It reached out to me, gesturing with its fingers for me to approach. "Come, join us." It smiled. "Join our legion and live forever."

The phantom took a tentative step towards me, making a harsh sound of metal scrapping on metal as small pieces of its foot adhered to the floor and almost broke away before drawing themselves back into the lumbering mass.

Its shrill laughter echoed down the corridor. Then it grinned and twisted its head a little. "I'm coming to get you." It took another step. "We're all coming to get you…"

I turned, raced up the stairs, and burst into the lab. My head reeled as I pushed the door shut and leaned against it while struggling to get my breath back.

Sandra lifted her head and croaked, "Phantom?"

I pulled down my mask, still too desperate for breath to speak properly, I nodded. Then it hit me. "You…" I raised my arm and pointed at her.

"What?"

"Your belly… the swelling… it's gone!"

"Swelling?" She looked at me as though I was a madman. "What are you talking about?"

"Before your last shot… your belly." How could she not know? "It had swelled out… really badly."

Speechless, Sandra placed a hand on her stomach, as though checking it was still there.

"I was worried." Breathing was still a struggle. "I was worried I'd get back from downstairs and find you'd become a hatchling too."

Sandra looked at me, bewilderment in her eyes. "But you still came back?"

I looked at the floor, embarrassed by the hopelessness of my answer. "There was nowhere else to go."

When I finally regained the courage to lift my gaze, she gave me a wry smile and let out a stifled laugh before shaking her head as she said, "Lucky eleven, huh? Who'd have thought? We'd best get online and spread the word."

"We can't. The net, it dropped out an hour or so ago."

She rubbed a hand against her forehead as though trying to relieve a headache. "Damn it!" She looked up. "I guess we should've known that was coming."

"It's worse than that." My voice trembled. "The phantom. It knew my name. It said they're coming for me."

"How much of Batch Eleven have we got?"

I knew the answer but counted again anyway before replying. "Five vials and a bottle with around a hundred mil that's growing at about ten mil an hour."

"It's not much, but it'll have to do." She glanced across at the window. There was a little over an hour of daylight left. "If it threatened you, we need to get out of here, now." Somehow, Sandra found the energy to swing her feet off the gurney. "We need to find somewhere safe that's hopefully still got some sort of net connection."

As she went to stand, her legs collapsed under the weight they'd become unaccustomed to supporting. I reached out and caught her under the shoulders before she hit the floor. "You need time to recover."

"We need to go."

The shrill maniacal laugh I'd heard downstairs erupted in the corridor outside the lab.

Sandra said, "Open one of the vials. Have it ready."

"What's that going to achieve?"

"Look at me. You said my belly had been swelling. Batch Eleven? It worked, Danny. It kills any nanobot it comes into contact with. It'll be like splashing acid in the phantom's face."

The door burst open and the laughter stopped. The phantom strolled into the lab, casually picking up spent vials and checking they were empty. It was wearing a blood-stained lab coat that it must have taken from its hatchling host. "Hello, Sandra… Danny." It looked at me, twisted its head, and grinned like it'd done downstairs. Sarcasm dripped off every word. "Why'd you run away?"

Sandra spoke through clenched teeth. "Leave him alone."

The shape of the phantom's face changed to match hers, the transition seeming as fluid as going from a grimace to a smile. "What's up, Doctor Wells?" It glanced around at the empty chairs scattered through the lab. "Is the woman who sold out humanity getting low on supporters?"

I held up a vial of Batch Eleven. "We've found the solution. You and your kind are history."

The phantom smiled at me. "Look at the face I'm wearing, Danny. This is the face of treachery. It's ironic. She's actually done humanity a favour, but that was just dumb luck.

A roll of the dice. A desperate gamble that she could save her son with an untested treatment."

I looked at her. "What's that about?"

Sandra snatched the vial from me, ripped its cap off in her teeth, and splashed its contents over the phantom. A metallic scream pierced my eardrums. The rancid smell of burning flesh and electronics assaulted our nostrils as the phantom tried to claw the soup of nanobots from its face.

Sandra tugged at my arm. "We have to go! Now!"

I grabbed my backpack from under the bench and shoved the bottle and vials of Batch Eleven into it. I put an arm under Sandra's shoulder and we moved as fast as we could toward the door. Although the phantom's eyes had burnt away, it still managed to reach out and grab my free arm, the pained screaming continuing as its grip tightened.

Out of the corner of her eye, Sandra spied the hammer on the bench. She stretched her arm out in the hope of getting a couple of fingers to it.

I tried to pull free of the creature's coarse grasp that was cutting into my forearm, but it wasn't letting go.

Sandra's fingers made contact with the end of the hammer's handle and dragged it close enough for her to get a better grip. The next instant she swung the hammer down through the phantom's shoulder, sending myriad scraps of broken flesh through the air.

The creature's dismembered arm clung to me as I dragged Sandra through the door and out into the corridor, the hammer still dangling from her hand. Pieces of the phantom's arm fell away as we ran from the lab. Its grip loosened, then it dropped to the floor in a pool of stinking slush. Compelled to reconnect with the rest of the parasitic monstrosity, it slithered away from us and back toward the lab.

I snatched the hammer from Sandra and didn't stop to look back until we were safely in the fire escape. Curiosity made me hold the door open for a moment and look back in the direction of the now distant shrieks. Satisfied the phantom wasn't in pursuit, I let the door close then sank to the cold concrete floor and tried to get my breath back.

Sandra said, "We need to keep moving."

"I need to rest."

Sandra shook her head. "We can't. The phantoms, they have a hive mind. Once the sun goes down and they wake up, they'll come after us. We're just lucky it was only a fresh hatchling we had to deal with back there."

"Is it true? What it said?"

"You can't trust what they say."

"But is it true?"

She used the railing to pull herself up. "I think I'll be right now. I can use this for support."

I waited on the floor for an answer.

Sandra started down the stairwell. "Come on, we need to find somewhere before dark."

She was two flights down by the time I got up and started after her. Sure that my first question would remain unanswered, I tried a different tack. "That phantom back there, what'll happen to it now?"

"Batch Eleven's virus will keep replicating and reaching into its cells, systematically disabling its nanobots until they're all destroyed."

"Can't it be restored to what it was before?"

Sandra stopped and looked back up the stairs as I tried to catch up. "What? To be human?" She looked down and shook her head. "The moment it hatched, all hope for that person was gone."

"But his consciousness, it was still there."

"No, his consciousness died when the phantom hatched. It's

a clean break. Having his memories and mimicking his thought patterns isn't the same as being a living human being."

It felt like I was drowning in a sea of lost hope as we continued down the stairs in silence. When I'd first arrived at the research institute wanting to help out, I'd been motivated by my belief that there was still a chance we could find a way to save the millions whose bloodied clothing hung outside almost every home as a warning.

The reality should have been obvious.

You just had to look at the shells left behind when the phantoms hatched.

Humans can be irrational.

We cling to false hopes.

And I'd just had mine laid bare in front of me, forcing me to grab hold of the only shred of hope left, that we may be able to save the small handful of humanity that hadn't yet succumbed to the phantom plague. Anxiety swept over me as the reality of that thought sank in.

Then the lights went out.

Sandra groaned, "Urgh, just what we didn't need. The generator must have shut down."

"You don't think it's them?"

"It can't be. Aside from fresh hatchlings, they don't come out until after dark."

"What if this one's already reached out to them? What if it told them they're under threat?"

Sandra pulled the phone from a pocket in her jeans. Her face looked eerie in its blueish light. "Speculating on worst case scenarios doesn't help."

Guided by her flashlight app, we were a couple of flights away from the bottom when we heard the distant creak of a door opening and the injured phantom's shrieking at the top of the stairwell.

Blood pulsed in my temples.

I put my arm around Sandra's shoulder and we raced down the remaining stairs.

We heard the clang of something above us bouncing on the metal handrails as it fell through the stairwell. A splash of organic matter and metal scratched against my cheek as a nondescript something fell past us. It's hard to say if it hit with a thud or a splat. Whatever it was, the sound echoed through the fire escape.

Sandra directed her phone so it illuminated the lab coat and pile of putrid mush at the stairwell's base.

To our mutual horror, the mush started to rise and fill the once white lab coat.

Adrenalin drove us forward, but it wasn't enough. We reached the bottom of the stairs only to have the phantom block our only possible exit.

Its face was a dancing mash of hideous distortion; its voice an electronic scream. "The liquid cancer, it burns. Make it stop!"

Fired up with determination, I lifted the hammer and began swinging wildly at the creature. Time and again, it tore through, momentarily breaking apart the magnetic bonds between nanobots that held the monstrosity together. The targeted areas became like a swarm of bees under the hammer's impact before rebinding after it had passed through.

The hatchling grabbed Sandra's shoulder and screeched, "Make it stop!"

I brought the hammer down hard on the elbow of the arm that held her. As soon as the connection was severed, Sandra fell back, taking the phantom's forearm with her.

I saw the chance and dragged her past the screaming hatchling, its detached arm still clutching her shoulder.

With the phantom lurching after us, we somehow made it to the door. A flash of lightning flooded the bottom of the stairwell as we pushed the door open and fell out into the tempest engulfing Sydney.

The hand groping Sandra's shoulder disintegrated and fell away. I looked back as we struggled through the downpour. There was no indication the phantom had tried to follow us outdoors.

If we wanted to find a working internet connection, the city centre would be our best hope. On a good day, the walk from the university campus to the city would take maybe twenty minutes. But it was a big ask to get there before dark while trying to work our way through one of the worst storms in living memory. To make it worse, we'd left our jackets in the lab.

My teeth chattered and I shivered in my saturated clothes.

Sandra had gone disturbingly silent.

We stumbled on regardless.

I don't know how long we'd walked by the time we reached the little shopping centre. A cord had been strung across its entrance with a bloody shirt pegged up in the standard warning not to enter. I pulled it down and dragged Sandra inside.

We'd found the antidote. We were safe from the plague's threat.

Ironically, in that moment I felt anything but safe. But the centre provided the opportunity to seek out food and warm clothing.

We stepped over puddles of mush and clothing, fully aware that less than an hour from now they would rise up as phantoms.

As we made our way toward a clothing store, Sandra's foot stumbled into one of the puddles, activating a reflex response.

A hand formed out of the pool of nanobots and cellular flesh. It grabbed her ankle.

I smashed down on the phantom limb with the hammer and we ran into a nearby Country Mountain Life outlet. Like most shops, the doors and windows had already been shattered.

I thought back to when the crisis began and everyone was so strong on taking a hard line against looters. Now, here we were, looting to survive.

Sandra was limp as I lifted her onto the counter. I pulled the blouse from her shoulder so I could inspect the damage where the phantom had grabbed her in the fire exit. The bruising was so severe that I suspected the bone may be fractured. She took hold of my wrist and whispered, "Just go on without me, or you'll never make it. You need to let the world know. We've found the antidote."

"I'm not going anywhere without you."

I rummaged through what little clothing was left in the store and found a couple of jackets that looked like they might fit us. I laid Sandra's over her like a blanket then leaned down and whispered in her ear, "I noticed a hole-in-the-wall grocery store next door. I'm going to see if I can find something to give us the energy to make it into town."

She grabbed my hand and squeezed it. "You do that."

It was slim pickings in the Anytime Grocery Store. The fruit and vegetables were all rotten and the rancid meat in the deli reminded me of the time I'd come across a rotting dog carcass on the roadside. It would have been easy to assume all the food within was contaminated, but there were still packets of biscuits in sealed wrappers that would be safe. I stuffed my backpack with as many as I could fit, then returned to where I'd left Sandra.

She was gone.

"SANDRA!" I called out as loud as I could, but there was no response. I walked out into the centre's arcade and called out again.

Still no response.

I leaned my back against a wall then felt my knees weakening as I slid down to the tiled floor. I didn't have the strength to do this, not on my own.

Tears flowed, the obligatory catharsis I knew I'd have to endure before it would be possible to re-evaluate my course of action.

I've no idea how much time had passed when the crack of thunder brought me back to my senses.

My backpack held the last chance for humanity's survival. Somehow, I had to let the world know, and if I had to do that on my own, then so be it.

I got to my feet and started walking again.

Despite my newly pilfered jacket, the driving rain cut through as though I'd been stripped naked.

I turned the corner from Goulburn into George Street.

Every balcony of every apartment block and every shop entrance displayed the same ominous warning, a clothesline with a single bloodied piece of clothing.

The wind picked up even more.

I worked my way north toward a precinct that held fond memories from my youth.

It was so different now.

The street was littered with abandoned cars and the remains of a broken helicopter that must have fallen from the sky when someone on-board erupted as a hatchling.

Even with the heavy rain and winds, the stench of rotting garbage piled up in the streets was an assault to the senses.

But then, a glimmer of hope. Outside the old cinema centre, fresh garbage lay at the top of the pile. The sight gave me extra strength to push on toward the venue of my earliest teenage dating experiences.

The wind eased by the time I reached the wall of glass doors that lined up to form the entrance. Most were boarded up, but there was one pair of inward opening doors that remained unobscured. As I got closer, I saw they were secured by heavy chains from the inside. More important than that, I could see signs of human activity deep inside the building.

I pushed myself against the glass to see. People were lining up where I'd lined up in box office queues as a kid.

They held bowls.

The cinema centre had become a soup kitchen.

I banged my fist on the doors and called out, "Let me in!"

A burly man with a bald head, a semi-automatic weapon slung over his shoulder, and wearing a surgical mask, approached the door. He pulled out a notepad and wrote on it, then pushed the page against the window.

You're not welcome here.

I pulled out my phone and wrote a response, then pulled one of the vials from my backpack and held them up to the window together.

I have the antidote.

He screwed his face up, then wrote another note and pressed it against the glass.

Why should I believe you?

I typed my response and held it up.

I've been working with Doctor Sandra Wells.

He stared at me for what felt like an eternity then walked away. A few minutes later, he returned with a woman wearing a nurse's uniform and surgical mask.

She pushed a note up against the glass.

Where did the plague originate?

The truth about the plague, that it was human created nanotech gone wrong, had never come out through the media. Conspiracy theorists had followed obscure tangents that were totally divorced from reality.

I typed my response and again held my phone up to the glass.

She read it then turned to the guard and nodded. He unlocked the chains and let them fall to the floor.

I pushed against the door and stepped inside as the guard shut the door behind me. Once he'd secured the padlock and chains the nurse suggested sealing the door off for the night.

The room became darker as he shifted the sheets of plywood to block all vision in or out.

My attention was fixed on the mindless procession of lost souls lining up for food.

"Give me your backpack," said the nurse.

"I can't."

She rolled her eyes, shook her head, and let out a sigh. "Just hand it over."

"I need an Internet connection."

"No, you need to give me your backpack."

The coldness of the guard's gun pressing against the back of my neck took me by surprise.

The nurse collected the backpack as I slipped it off my shoulders.

"Sister will see you now."

She turned and led me up the stairs. Although the staircase was several metres wide, there was only a narrow passageway through the sea of corpse-like figures that lay on the stairs, either moaning in a semi-conscious state or staring blankly into space.

I'd witnessed a scene like this before.

When I was a teenager and desperate to score some smoke, a housemate had taken me to his place of last resort for scoring pot... a shooting gallery. It was a pitiful collection of a few dozen lost souls, controlled by the only human being in the place with lucid eyes. He turned out to be a barrister... a Queen's Counsel no less. Apparently, he revelled in the control he had over the inhabitants who lay sprawled out on soiled mattresses throughout the pathetic Kings Cross basement.

This seemed no different.

I reached the top of the second flight of stairs and was confronted by the gallery's queen. She sat in a butchered cinema seat, her decrepit pseudo throne. She leaned forward and cradled her chin in her hands. Like the others who controlled this place, she hid behind a surgical mask. "So, you're a friend of Doctor Wells… the Nobel Laureate and traitor to humanity?"

"I wouldn't say that I'm her friend, I've only known her for two weeks." I paused as I thought about just how little I'd come to know her in that time. "I'd sought her out to see if there was anything I could do to help her try to find a cure. And we found it. We found an antidote."

"Cold comfort to everyone who's already dead."

I had no answer.

"Tell me, did she confess the truth to you… of how she betrayed humankind?"

The question felt like an accusation. "No, I'd heard nothing of that till an hour or so ago when we were confronted by a phantom hatchling. It accused her, but I don't know anything more than that."

"Where is she now?"

"I don't know. We left the UTS research facility together. She needed to rest, so I went scavenging for food. When I got back, she was gone."

The queen opened my backpack that the nurse hand left at her feet. She pulled out a vial and held it up to the light. "So, are you telling me this is humanity's last hope, your antidote?"

"The nanobots in the liquid are designed to seek out and destroy any other nanotech that's embedded in human cells. It works. I've seen it firsthand."

She stared at me, her mouth and nostrils hidden behind her mask, leaving just her eyes to interrogate me as she asked, "What's your name?"

"Daniel… Daniel Rhodes. Most people call me Danny."

"Tell me, Daniel Rhodes. This antidote of yours, does it self-replicate?"

"Yes."

She threw her hands in the air and pulled down her mask so I could see her full face. "There-in lies the problem. Fighting one self-replicating technology with another. That's how we got here in the first place isn't it? All cancers self-replicate and all that self-replicates is cancer." She rose to her feet and held the vial out toward me. "One stupid researcher decides it's safe to fight the cancer invading her son with her own version of a self-replicating curse, triggering the end of humanity as we know it."

"It works, I've seen it."

"But it replicates. Like everything that replicates, it will mutate. It's just another cancer. Think about it, dozens of trillions of cells in a human body. What are the odds of copying every one of those without a glitch; a mutation? Mutations are radical enough when they come from nature. Ask yourself, how reliable has digital technology been? When's the last time you came across a glitch-free software update?" She handed the vial to the nurse and said, "Destroy it, along with whatever else might be in his bag."

"No!" I reached out for the backpack, but a multitude of hands grabbed hold of my arms and pulled them behind my back.

She turned back to me. "Humanity's finished. It didn't take long after our community congregated here for us to see the truth. Now, we try to make the end as peaceful for those who are left as we can." She gestured toward the human wrecks occupying the stairway. "Pacified masses are easier to control. So we raided nearby clinics and police stations for whatever opiates we could find. My subjects are happy in their blissful ignorance that the end is near." She took a step back toward her throne, silhouetted by the fading light beyond the wall of windows behind her, then struck a pose that seemed almost regal. "And for one miserable moment in my life, I get to be in control."

"The cure works."

The queen turned to the security guard. "I've had enough. Throw him out. It's getting dark. Let the phantoms do with him what they will."

*

Freda looked at the vials laid out on the lab bench.

It was six months since the virus released by Doctor Wells in her dying days had mutated.

Now, having been forced to watch so many of her fellow hatchlings succumb to the nano-cancer, it had infected her as well.

Despite the collective intelligence of the hive mind, it was hard to choose which vial from the trial medications to inject.

This was supposed to be humanity's future, the next stage in our evolution, but every decision so far from the hive had been flawed, especially when dealing with the nano-cancer virus.

The hive was adamant.

She should go with Batch Seven.

Unconvinced, she opened the drawer and pulled out the dice.

It felt so good to place her faith in blind luck.

She closed her eyes and rolled the dice.

Five and six.

Homo Imperfectus

by

Peter Mark Lewis

Professor Straightman stared with disbelief at the document in her hand. Long perfect fingers began to tremble, making the sheet of metapaper flutter like a startled butterfly.

She swung to face the man sitting on the opposite side of her desk, and roared: 'You can't be serious!'

He flinched, though it was obvious he had anticipated her reaction. He cleared his voice and replied simply: 'Very serious.'

The professor groped for words to describe her consternation, but none came out. Frustrated, she sought a reprieve from the document itself, scanning it several times for errors or evidence of fraud. But, to her disgust, there was nothing - the seal of the science council was plainly visible on the bottom, along with the chairman's signature. If this was a fake then it was a masterful one.

'You realise,' she said through clenched teeth, 'What this means, don't you?'

'Of course,' the man replied with a shrug, his handsome face a picture of self-control. His eyes belied the outward display of diffidence, however, by darting about the office.

The professor leaned across her desk as if to capture his wandering irises. 'So, Mister...'

'Citizen, Norm Citizen. Bioplanning administrator, class one.'

'So, Mister... Citizen, you're prepared to take full responsibility for this... this... experiment of yours?'

'I'd hardly call it an experiment but yes, I'm prepared to accept full responsibility. Mind you, I can't take credit for the concept itself. That honour goes to a philoso-researcher at MIT way back in 2237. I'm merely the first person to see a need for it.'

'A need for it? You must be joking. Since when does a need exist for abominations.'

Citizen shook his head in irritation. 'Really Professor, this is an old argument, and one I've had many times with various conservative members of the council. I'd hoped for a less ancient debate from someone as learned as yourself...'

'Ancient! That's an ironic choice of words, isn't it? You're the person who's planning to bring history back to life, Mister Bioplanning Administrator Class One. Resurrecting the nameless horrors of the past will look very elegant on your job description - after you've been impeached for genetic desecration.' She leaned back and crossed her arms. 'Though doubtless, like all bureaucrats, you've got some contingency plan to cover yourself if this experiment goes wrong. Presumably I'll get the blame instead.'

She looked down at the document one more time then discarded it to the floor with a dramatic sweep of her hand. A spidery micro-cleaner emerged from beneath the desk, snatched the sheet and disposed of it in a recycling slot. The metapaper was devoured in a flash of light, council seal and all.

'I'm sorry,' said Citizen with a look of weariness, 'That you feel this way about the program. It would've been much better if you were a willing participant. And your cynicism about the council is undeserved, they were aware of the ramifications and debated the pros and cons for some time. In the end, however, they were unanimous.'

'Oh? Well, if the council's so sure about their decision, why delegate somebody else to do their dirty work? I wasn't even consulted. There must have been several genomists on the discussion board who could carry out this procedure.'

'Yes, three to be precise, but none with your qualifications or obstetric experience. We want you to oversee this case beyond conception. Beyond birth too for that matter.'

The professor's large brown eyes widened into a look of horror.

Citizen continued, 'You're to follow the first three years of this child's development. Possibly more if all goes well. And you're to report personally to the council on the subject's progress: emotional responses, creative tendencies, anything that might be out of the ordinary. We have high hopes for this individual.'

'But... but... I can't possibly...'

'Is it a matter of payment? The council have assured me you'll be well credited, and if this is a success then you'll have full publishing rights as well. Just think of the royalties on a story like this! Twenty Third Century Fox will probably make a simulation about it.' He stifled a chuckle. 'Hopefully with someone good-looking playing my role.'

Professor Straightman reacted with a humourless huff. The irony of the young bureaucrat's remark had not escaped her. He was a model of physical perfection: handsome, pearl-skinned and robust. In a previous era he would have been an easy choice for an acting career – a starring role for that matter. But in this utopian age he was just another person.

'I suspect,' said the professor, 'They'll probably use a g-twelve for your part. If they want to stick to reality, that is.'

Citizen blinked at her in amazement.

She smiled at his discomfort. 'You are a caucasoid g-twelve, are you not?'

The man blinked again. 'How did you know?'

'How could I not know,' replied the professor with an air of superiority. 'I'm a DNA Patterner, remember? You're a superseded model, but I never forget a face. We made scores of your genotype back in the fifties. Very popular for a while there - until negroid variant m-fifty nine was developed, that is.' Her expression became devious. 'Ah yes... *m-fifty nine*. Now there was a real fad! We just couldn't conceive enough of those babies. Taller, so-o-o charming, and much more intelligent...'

'I think we're digressing from the subject,' said Citizen, looking nettled. 'If you're using your knowledge to score cheap points off me then you're just wasting both our times. I've come here in person to facilitate your willing involvement, not to be insulted.'

Straightman rolled one of her neat hands into a fist and banged it on the desk. 'The only insult around here is the council's demand, it's a breach of professional ethics. You're ordering me to make a monster on purpose, after a lifetime of producing ideal human beings! Well, I'm sorry to disappoint them, but I won't do it.'

'I'm afraid it's a little beyond that already. Burning a sheet of metapaper won't save you from their directive. If you fail to comply then you'll be dismissed.'

'I'm aware of that.' She leaned back in the leather expanse of the genomaster chair, her expression defiant.

'Loss of pay,' he continued, 'reduction of privileges. Are you sure you want that as well?'

She shrugged.

Citizen pondered her for a moment then said: 'The prospective mother of this child is quite willing, you realise.'

'What? It's to be a full surrogacy? Surely no woman would want such a thing!'

'Natural gestation is a key part of this program, a foetal tank might neutralise some of the eccentricity we're hoping for. You may be surprised to know it wasn't hard to find a woman prepared to help us. In fact she's looking forward to it.'

'Ridiculous. Has she been properly briefed?'

'Of course,' Citizen replied, becoming indignant. 'I'm not in the business of deceit, professor. The entirety of this program is public domain, and registered in the science council's directory under: 'New Initiatives'. Look it up if you want to.'

'Don't worry,' she replied, narrowing her eyes, 'I will - in great detail.'

'Good. Does this mean you might be helping us then?'

'I didn't say that!' She closed her hand into a fist again, but this time refrained from hitting the desk. 'Have I missed something here? Has the world turned upside down since I ascended to Chief of Genomistry? It appears that all those well-formed babies I helped create have grown up to become a sea of... of... ingrates. Forget beauty and intelligence, aberration is the latest virtue! A fad, I suppose, like all the others.' She opened her hand and looked down at it, her expression dejected.

'Professor, I can understand your feelings and be assured I'm not in the business of servicing social whims.' He leaned toward her, his expression conciliatory. 'You can be justifiably proud of the work you've done, and mankind has been irrevocably improved. We're healthier, smarter, better in almost every way. But...'

'But? But what? What can be better than perfection?'

'There's an ancient moral that says: 'Don't throw babies out with the bathwater.' And over the last two centuries a lot of very acceptable baby designs have been discarded in our genetic clean-out. Many character traits have been entirely swept away.'

The professor's demeanour became combative. 'Babies? Bathwater? You lecture me with an ancient moral? If memory serves me correctly, Mr Citizen, the ancients had little in the way of morals. And some of those character traits you glorify were design flaws that even our ancestors despised.' She turned to a console and muttered a brief command. At once the top of her desk became a lit screen, and at the centre of it lay an enlarged copy of the science council's directive. After a glance at its details, the professor returned her attention to Citizen. 'In fact, this particular trait you want to bring back was so reviled by the ancients they eliminated it at the dawn of genomic restructuring. Some of their descriptions of it make interesting reading too, with words such as 'unnatural', 'deviant' and 'perverted'. Need I go on?'

Citizen shifted in his chair and his eyes resumed their wandering about the office, observing the micro-cleaners as they bustled about their work. They were the same shade of beige as the office, and sported Genomistry logos on their crab-like carapaces.

The bureaucrat cleared his throat and continued, his words coming out measured and patient.

'Professor, the most obvious is always the most overlooked. I prefer to think that we're filling in some of the gaps left by the initial rush of perfection-seekers. And where better to start but at the beginning, with the most famous eccentricity of all.'

'Hah! Like all bureaucrats, the only real mastery you possess is one of euphemism. What possible value could this particular eccentricity have?'

Citizen studied the woman's smooth eurasian face. He knew from her records that she was close to seventy yet she appeared to be in her thirties, and like himself was as flawless as an icon.

He considered for a moment then said: 'May I see your hand? Your right one?'

She hesitated at first, unsure of his motive, then shrugged and held it out toward him. 'Be my guest.'

He took the offering and held it gently, as if it were an elegant bird. 'I noticed earlier that you have superb extremities - if I may be so bold.'

'You may, and thankyou for the compliment. I'm an asianoid b-twenty four. My parents chose me with great care, and I'm very proud of my genetic designation. All b-twenty fours have beautiful limbs.'

'Yes,' Citizen replied, 'doubtless.' He turned her hand over to reveal the palm. The flesh was as smooth as the topside, with a minimum of creases.

'You know,' he continued, 'in pre-genomic times there was an art-form called palmistry, where a person's personality and fate were said to be revealed in the lines on their hands.'

'Yes, I know. A childish preoccupation.' Her tone became sarcastic. 'Is that something you plan to revive as well?'

'Only if our new creation wishes it.' He ran his eyes over the soft suede skin. 'Such an art would be pointless in this day and age however, since no-one has a unique pattern any more.' He laid his own white hand next to hers. It was equally devoid of signature lines.

The professor sniffed. 'I suppose you're trying to make a point with all this.'

'You could say that,' he replied, contemplating their upraised fingers. 'Did you know there was another art that genetics swept away? Well, a science actually... fingerprinting.'

'Of course, an early form of criminal identification. Is this another history lesson?'

Citizen ignored her jibe. 'Have a close look at the ends of my fingers. See anything?'

The professor leaned forward to peer, but saw only smooth ivory flesh. Even his fingernails were perfect.

'No,' she replied with a dismissive tone. 'Was I supposed to?'

'Now look at yours. See anything?'

She sighed and repeated the procedure. 'No, nothing. So what's to see?'

'Nothing is the right answer. We have no fingerprints, at least not in the original sense. Just a small amount of texture to provide grip.'

'So?'

'Don't you get it? We're like these micro-cleaners around your office. Our bodies vary slightly but the inner workings are almost identical. And like them we tend to behave the same way.'

As if on cue, a cleaner meandered across the broad expanse of the desk, fastidiously polishing away their fingermarks as it went. Professor Straightman frowned and crossed her arms as Citizen continued.

'Don't believe me? Who's your favourite artist? I'll bet it's Michelangelo.'

She grimaced. 'Mr Citizen, I hope you haven't been reading my personal files...'

'Of course not. Think of it as a lucky guess. Tell me, what's your favourite form of relaxation?'

'Experiencing simulations.'

'Ditto, and what's your favourite sim.'

'Really, I fail to see...'

'It's 'Queen of Paradise', isn't it?'

The Professor reddened. 'How did you know?'

'Call it a coincidence. My own favourite, by the way, is King of Paradise. Did you know that all genotypes born after the year 2219 list those sims as their favourites? Another coincidence? You tell me.'

'Are you saying that it's wrong for everybody to prefer a particular sim?'

'No, but it lacks variance. In former centuries no two people had the same tastes. Now we're in a time when no two people have different tastes. Ever noticed how popular the colour beige is? Or ballet? Or opera? Two centuries ago those preferences were the exception, now they're the rule.' Citizen leaned back in his chair and smiled to himself. 'I suspect old Genomaster Pyotr Kaminsky had a bit to do with it, he always did like to put something of himself into his work. And he was a serious man with serious tastes.'

The professor paused to consider the young bureaucrat's words for a moment, her mind hunting for a flaw in his argument.

'If,' she replied at last, 'what you say is true, then why are we arguing? Everybody should be in complete agreement about everything.'

'It's not that simple. As you know, we're all designed to carry out different functions. Take me for example: G-twelves are designed for bureaucratic work, since we never tire of repetition. Your job, however, needs a good deal of academic intellect, and what better than a b-twenty four for such a task. These minor variations mean we don't share the same viewpoints.'

'Hence we can still argue. Fair enough, but I still don't see why we need to reintroduce abomination.'

'Ah, such a dramatic use of language. Let's just say we're returning a wild card to a dull game, and hopefully this person will provide us with a more unique perspective.'

'I take your point, but really, this defect of all of them. I mean… look at it.'

She touched her console, and the projected copy of the council directive expanded until it spread-eagled the entire desk. With a stroke of her hand the words in question became emblazoned in red.

Citizen looked at them but his demeanour remained unchanged. He replied: 'This abomination, as you call it, professor, has a noble lineage. Some of the greatest and brightest in history have shared it.'

'Rubbish! Name one.'

'Oscar Wilde.'

'Ha! A perfect example to support my case. The poor fellow was consumed by scandal when his imperfections were found out, and he died in obscure misery.'

'Your knowledge of history makes you a worthy challenger. How about Alexander of Macedonia?'

'A butcher and tyrant.'

'Hm,' said Citizen in mock contemplation, 'No point using Shaka Zulu as my next example then. Let's shift to the arts, and where better to start than Michelangelo himself.'

'Surely you jest!

'Sorry, it's common knowledge.'

The professor winced. 'Not so common that I knew about it.'

'Look it up if you doubt me. Historians believe it was an integral part of his genius, and he was in good company. About one in every fifteen ancients possessed this same flaw.'

'Inconceivable.'

'Actually, I'd describe them now as unconceivable, thanks to the science of Genomistry. But, with a little help from you...' He looked at her hopefully.

She raised an eyebrow. 'I'm not promising anything. At least, not until I've researched the background to this case. I'll want full dataflow before I make a decision, and I won't be bullied into it by anybody. Is that understood?'

'Loud and clear. I take it then that your 'refusal' has been renegotiated to a 'maybe'?'

'Take it any way you like. In the interests of science I'm reserving any personal feelings, and my final decision will be based on impartial analysis.'

Citizen smiled in an unabashed display of gratitude. 'I could ask for no fairer hearing than that.' He stood up and outstretched his hand. 'Chief Genomaster Vera Straightman, I bid you good day.'

She took his fingers in hers, shook them crisply and said, 'I'll let you know my decision soon. There is one thing however...' Her expression changed to one of embarrassed puzzlement.

'Yes?' replied Citizen.

'Hm, it's a silly thing really, but it's just as well not to overlook it. This individual you intend to create... assuming, that is, I give my approval...'

'Yes,' he replied a second time, his smile giving way to a look of concern.

The professor continued: 'Is it wise that this creature should be created in isolation? It is, after all, a deviant from the norm. Shouldn't we consider... I mean, it is different, with its own rather peculiar physical and er... sexual needs...'

'Quite so.' The bureaucrat bit his lip in anticipation.

'Well, won't it be necessary to make another one? To provide it with... um, company?' Her cheeks reddened.

Citizen looked stunned for a moment, then leaned his head back and laughed with delight.

'As you wish,' he replied, barely able to stop himself from shaking. 'I leave the rest of this program in your hands. It's been a pleasure meeting you, my dear Genomaster.'

And with that he bowed deeply, turned on his heel and departed.

The professor's eyes watched him go but her thoughts were elsewhere, still nurturing a secret doubt. She activated the console and opened some key files. By the time the young bureaucrat's footsteps had finished echoing down the hall, a major weakness had been found in his argument. Or, to be more precise, a major weakness had been found in the bureaucrat himself.

She leaned back in her chair and let out a long slow sigh. It was an exhalation of air that had no savour of victory, rather a weary tone of sadness. Once she presented her findings to the council, the good Mister Citizen and his whole hair-brained experiment would be sidelined without further debate.

A microbot ambled across the smoothness of the desk, its tiny vacuum head skittering from side to side in an eternal search for grime - a pointless exercise since untidiness was one of the human eccentricities that genomists had eliminated.

Professor Straightman rapped her long perfect fingers on the glass top of the desk, leaving tiny fingermarks as she did so. The circular smudges were even, featureless, and swiftly removed by the darting nose of the cleaner.

She pondered the tiny machine as it went about its work. With its methodical attention to detail and its Genomaster logo proudly displayed, it might have been an insect copy of herself: another glamorous desk-polisher, smug in its perfection and diligence, and so dull that it was not even aware of its dullness.

The professor's eyes returned to the info-display. There, in synopsis, lay Norm Citizen's own DNA structure.

His flaw was exactly as she suspected. Normally, caucasoid g-twenty fours were designed for administrative functions and were rather tedious fellows, and certainly not prone to Citizen's outrageous flights of fancy. To a scientist like her, familiar with the various genotypes, it was obvious from the start that the poor fellow was suffering an abnormality. And there on the desk display was the proof: a DNA flaw from a bygone era - the very same aberration he was so heavily endorsing. Little wonder then that he wanted to produce miscreants, he was merely attempting to reproduce himself. A plan she was about to thwart.

Her elegant index finger moved to the 'Directive Denied' icon and hovered there while she considered the man and his argument.

It was remarkable that such a profoundly flawed individual had been created, but genomics was still a complex art. The resulting kink inside Citizen's brain had also given him a rare persuasive power; since his verbal skills had seduced the entire council. In an ironic way, he was living proof of his own theory. Eccentricity did have its compensations.

An ancient proverb came to mind: In an insane land only the mad are sane.

The professor wavered for a moment then chided herself for entertaining such doubts. Now was the time for decisive action, no more vacillation. She took a deep breath, pressed downward, and her smooth fingertip activated the icon marked: 'Directive Approved.'

She looked with astonishment at her own action, as if unable to comprehend what her hand had just done. The document disappeared and a geno-interface took its place. Somewhere in the bowels of the institute a tiny ovum was being prepared for insemination, its DNA code awaiting the final encryption.

Professor Straightman recovered from her initial surprise, and felt for the first time the godlike powers that science had thrust upon her. She and her fellow genomists had been tampering with creation itself for generations. And to what end? Had they succeeded or failed? Who could say, for without an objective observer there was no way of knowing.

She suddenly understood why instinct had guided her finger to the approval button. Here was an opportunity for scientists to find out once and for all if the pursuit of perfection was folly, by creating individuals unlike themselves on purpose. Comparison would then supply the final answers.

Armed with fresh resolve, her long fingers moved swiftly over the display, calibrating the chromosomal structure to fine detail. An hour later she came at last to the encryption point where the fault would have to be inserted. The professor paused again in minor indecision, this time not from scientific doubt but from a simple inadequacy of spelling. The computer required a descriptive noun in the icon box. She knew the common name of this eccentricity, of course, but was it written as one word, two words, or two words hyphenated? The impasse was solved when she remembered that the computer would correct spelling mistakes anyway.

To savour the moment's historic importance the professor used her right index finger to type it in one letter at a time, then leaned back to contemplate the result. Before her lay the title of mankind's most famous idiosyncrasy, not seen in many centuries. A hundred years hence it might be enjoying a renaissance, along with many other human foibles. Genomists might even invent new ones.

Professor Straightman thought of a wry name to describe this new wave of humanity: 'Homo Imperfectus.' She smiled with amused satisfaction as the computer launched the program, carrying with it the once dreaded description: *left-handed.*

No Good Deed

by

Erin Munzenberger

It all happened so fast. Kels was driving. It was one of those grey and dreary afternoons where the whole world seems muted. It wasn't raining now, but it had earlier, and the streets were slick and wet. Everything around her was oddly still and silent; hers was the only car in sight. No pedestrians hurried past on the footpath; no children played in the park ahead.

\Kels wasn't rushing. She was going down a steep hill, and her mother didn't raise no fools. Still, one moment the road ahead was clear. She blinked, and suddenly the dog was there - loping right up the centre line towards her car, its red tongue lolling out of its mouth, yellow eyes gleaming against its jet-black coat. Kels shrieked out 'shit!' and hit the brakes.

The car didn't stop. She heard the tyres squealing, clutched the wheel with white-knuckled hands as the car skidded on the wet, down the hill, and smack into the dog. Its cut-off scream sliced into the air as the dog disappeared beneath the car, and Kels felt the crunch as it went underneath the tyre.

Finally, the car slid to a stop. She couldn't see the dog in her mirrors. Shaking, Kels threw the car into park, pulled on the handbrake, and spilled out of the door. Her legs felt like jelly as she stumbled up the length of her car, rounded the boot, and saw the limp, black huddle lying on the asphalt. Thin streaks of blood were running in the water on the road, reaching for her like accusing hands. With her breath coming in sharp, staccato gasps, Kels ran to the dog, and dropped to her knees beside it.

It wasn't dead. Oh God, it wasn't dead! Its front paws scraped futilely at the surface of the road, as if it was trying to get to its feet, but its back end was mauled; a twisted, bloody tangle. It fixed Kels with those yellow eyes, desperate and frightened, and the air shivered with its pleading whine.

'Oh.' She sobbed as she put her arms around it. Kels lifted as best she could, weeping afresh as the animal cried out in pain. It was so heavy. She didn't know what breed it was - from the shape of it, she might have said a German Shepherd, but it was larger again than any German Shepherd she had ever seen, and black all over, like spilled ink. Somehow, Kels managed to get it to her car, and laid it as gently as she could into the backseat. The dog lay there, crying.

'I know, baby, I know. I'm sorry.' Kels had to move her car. It was still in the middle of the road - she was lucky she hadn't been mowed down by someone coming up behind her, slipping in the wet just as she had. She pulled the car over to the side of the road and fumbled her phone out of her bag with shaking fingers. Kels googled the nearest vet and rang the number. Their website declared it was emergencies only, being a Sunday.

'Hello?'

'Oh, thank God!' She was all but hysterical. 'Please, I've hit a dog - it just came out of nowhere! Can you help me?'

The voice on the other end of the line was calm, cool, and advised her to take a deep breath. They would meet her there.

Did she have the address? She did. She dropped the phone when she tried to hang up, and left it lying on the floor of the car.

It was a miracle Kels didn't have another accident driving to the vet's. She couldn't stop looking in the rear-view mirror at the dog. Its eyes met hers every single time, boring into her: begging, accusing. God.

'You just came out of nowhere,' she heard herself saying, wracked with guilt. 'It wasn't my fault. You came out of nowhere.'

The dog did not absolve her.

The vet was getting out of her car, one of those squishy little SUVs, when Kels pulled into the parking lot. Another car followed her in, a second woman getting out - the nurse/admin/ assistant lady, Kels would soon learn. They strode over together and looked at the dog in the back of Kels' car.

'Jesus, he's huge. Okay, let's get him inside quickly.' The nurse ran to get a blanket. Between the three of them they somehow managed to get the dog into it and haul him inside like he was on a stretcher. He cried pitifully all the way. Once he was on the table, Kels expected to be shooed back to the waiting room, but it seemed that the vet and the nurse were too busy to bother with her, so she simply stood back out of the way, trying to be as quiet and unobtrusive as possible.

The nurse had a scanner and ran it over the dog while the vet examined his injuries.

'No chip,' the nurse reported.

'I'll pay for it.' Kels didn't know what made her say it. It wasn't her dog. She hadn't meant to hurt it. She would never deliberately harm an animal.

'If he doesn't have an owner, I mean. I'll pay for his treatment, if -'

If you can save him. The words died in her throat. The vet nodded, brisk, business-like.

'Okay. Well, this needs an x-ray. This leg looks broken, and I think we may be dealing with a dislocated hip.' She started rattling off orders to the nurse.

'Then … he's not going to die?'

The vet looked up at Kels, then, and smiled.

'No. No, I'll need to see the x-rays, of course, but, at this stage, I think the worst-case scenario will probably be needing to put a pin in his leg.'

A wave of relief slammed down on Kels so hard that she actually sat down on the floor. She felt like laughing hysterically.

'Oh my God,' she gasped out. 'I thought I'd killed him.'

'Nah, said the vet, ruffling the dog's ears. He whined and tried to lick her hand. 'Not even close.'

*

'Here he is!' The vet nurse - her name was Rebecca - held the door to the waiting room open. Kels stood as the dog - her dog, now - hobbled out, his leg in a cast. He stopped still when he saw her, ears back, tail low. She held out her hand, and he slunk forward a couple of cautious steps to sniff at her. When he smelt the treat clenched in her fist his ears perked up and his tail twitched. She opened her hand, the treat offered on her upturned palm, and he snatched it, wolfing it down. Kels felt his canines scrape against her skin.

'Who's a good boy?' Rebecca cooed. 'He's been such a sweetie, really. Any idea what you're going to call him?'

'Honestly, I haven't got a clue.' Kels crouched down to ruffle the dog's ears. He stared at her with those unnerving yellow eyes until she looked away, towards Rebecca. 'Everything I could think of was sort of cutesy, and he's really… not.'

'Oh, but he is handsome. Yes, you are. Yes, you are.' Kels noticed that the dog wagged his tail properly for her. Which was fair enough, Kels supposed. She was the nasty lady who had hit him with a car.

'Well, let us know when you bring him back for his next appointment,' Rebecca was saying. 'And once that leg's all better, the vet wanted to talk to you about,' she lowered her voice to a whisper, mimed a scissor action.

'- snip, snip.'

The dog barked.

They got out to Kels' car alright, and Rebecca helped her hoist the dog into the backseat without jarring his injured leg. The dog got himself out once they got home, nearly bowling Kels over in the process, and spent a good hour thoroughly exploring her house and small yard, and all the things she'd bought for him over the past two days - a bed, bowls, toys. He sniffed things, peed on things - all outside, thankfully - dog stuff. Kels gave him some of the dry food she'd got from the vet, hid his evening tablet in a piece of frankfurt, and nearly lost a finger giving it to him.

She wouldn't have to take him for walks just yet, but it was something she was seriously worried about.

I'll hire a trainer, she thought. Just for a few ses*sions,* to give me some pointers.

Kels ate her dinner in the lounge room with the telly on. The dog stretched out on the carpet at her feet, head up, apparently watching The Fall as raptly as she was. When bedtime rolled around he seemed reluctant to move, so she gave him a pat, murmured: 'goodnight boy,' and left him where he was.

*

Kels had the most awful dream. She was lying on an asphalt road that stretched endlessly in either direction. There was nothing on either side but grey ash. The sky was the same dirty yellow colour as an old bruise. Her hair whipped in a hot, stinking wind.

Her legs were a smashed, pulpy mess.

The pain was indescribable - so bad that she couldn't even scream. Her palms burned when she put them against the asphalt, tried to push herself up. She could hear her spilled blood sizzling, smelled the stench of copper and charred flesh wafting into the air.

A distant rumble. The blare of a horn, so loud it left the ground shaking. Kels looked up, and saw the truck screaming towards her, all glaring lights and menacing chrome.

'Nn- nn- nn.'

She tried to wave her arms, tried to make the driver see her there, but the truck just kept coming.

'Nn- no. No!'

With the metal behemoth just metres away, Kels turned her face against her shoulder, and finally found the breath to scream.

*

She jerked awake with a shuddering gasp. The first thing Kels saw was a pair of yellow eyes staring at her from out of the pitch black.

She screamed. Then she remembered the dog.

He was standing over her, unmoving. She sat up and let out a long breath.

'Oh, shit. What are you doing, boy? You scared me.'

The dog blinked slowly.

Kels rubbed her hands over her face. When she looked up again, the dog simply turned around, limped over to the other side of the room, and lay down. Kels sat and watched him for a while - as best as one can watch a black dog in the dark - until the rise and fall of his breathing had slowed, and she was reasonably certain he had gone to sleep. Only then did she lay back herself and stare up at the ceiling until dawn.

*

'What about ... Morpheus?' Adam, Kels' brother, was seated on the floor, squeaking a bright red rubber bone at the dog. In response, the dog simply sat there, staring like a sphinx.

'Mmm ... nah. Can you imagine walking around the park, yelling: 'Morpheus! Morpheus!' People would think I was strange.'

'You are strange, Kels. That's why this weird dog suits you.' Adam tossed the bone lightly at the dog's front paws. It landed with a soft *thwump*. The dog didn't so much as blink.

'Gee, thanks.'

'You didn't scramble his brain when you hit him, did you?'

'I dunno … maybe?' Kels brought two cups of coffee out of the kitchen, handed one to her brother, and took a seat on the couch.

'He seemed normal enough at the vet's.' She wrapped her hands around her mug and crossed her legs. 'How about Poe?'

'Like … from Star Wars?'

'No! Idiot. As in Edgar Allen.'

'How is shouting 'Poe!' in a crowded park any less strange than shouting 'Morpheus!'?'

'Yeah, fair point.' She took a sip of coffee, tapped the cup against her lip.

'Nothing I try seems to suit him. Darcy. Heathcliff. Jack.'

Adam snorted.

'I saw this video on YouTube of a lady who rescued a cat from traffic and called it 'Skid Mark'.'

'I am not calling my dog 'Skid Mark'.'

'Cujo?'

'God, no.'

*

'Come on, Dog. Here, boy.' Kels rattled the food bowl.

'Din dins.'

The dog shuffled in, nails clicking lightly against the tiled floor. Kels put the bowl back on the kitchen counter and grabbed her pre-prepared drug stuffed frankfurt.

'Okay, pill time, and then you can have your bickies. Siiiit.'

The dog did not sit. Kels had looked up a number of training videos on YouTube, and read countless articles on Google, and she was confident that she was doing everything right. Pushing down gently on the dog's backside didn't work. Holding a treat close under his nose until he backed up so much he sat down didn't work either. The dog never moved. He just … stared at her.

It was getting really frustrating.

'Alright, Mister. Now, look here. You need to eat this sausage. I know you *want* to eat this sausage. But I'm not going to give it to you until you *sit.*'

Nothing happened. Then, without warning, the dog launched himself at Kels.

She shrieked as wickedly sharp fangs plunged into her hand, sliding through skin and flesh like staples through paper. Kels fell backwards on her ass, the dog on top of her, smacking back against the kitchen cupboards hard enough to ring her bell. A hot mix of blood and drool slid down her arm, the smells of copper and hairy beast smothering her.

The frankfurt fell from her grip.

Like that, the dog let her go. He snuffled up the frankfurt, then turned back to look at her. He barked, wagged his tail, and treated Kels to a doggy grin - with her blood still dripping from his muzzle.

Shocked to her core, she looked down at her hand. Dark red welled from the semi-circle of deep puncture-tears on the back of the appendage. One of her fingers twitched spasmodically. The blood dripped down, pattering onto her legs and the white kitchen tile, spreading across the floor far faster than Kels would ever have believed possible. There was just so much of it.

The dog sat down across from her, tilted his head to the side, and lolled his tongue out happily.

*

Kels' Mum pulled her car into the driveway. For a moment her headlights shone over the lounge room window, the curtains still open. Kels saw the amber gleam of the dog's eyes as the lights passed over them where he stood inside.

Her Mum saw them too.

'Sweetheart, I don't think you should go back in there. Let me take you back to my place. I've got things you can wear. I just don't think that animal is safe.'

Kels looked down at her hand, wrapped in a swathe of bandages. She'd had to have stitches, but the doctor she had seen in Emergency felt that she had probably avoided any serious problems like nerve damage. Still, there would have to be tests.

'Thanks, Mum. But … I think it was my fault. I knew he was snatchy, and I was waving the frankfurt around in front of his face. He shouldn't be blamed for my stupidity.'

Her Mum didn't say anything. Kels could see the strain in her face.

'I'll be fine, I promise. Thanks for taking me to the hospital.'

*

Kels' boss had okayed her working from home. He'd asked if she wanted a few days off, but the team's deadline was next Friday, and Kels would be damned if she was going to let the side down. They'd sent her a fruit basket and the world's cheesiest get-well card.

It was awkward typing with just one hand, but she was making steady progress: sifting through emails, sending reports, editing documents, when the dog started to bark. Really bark. Kels could have sworn that the whole house was shaking with the force of it. She could feel the sound waves bouncing painfully around in her skull.

'Holy shit.' She clapped her hands over her ears and hurried to go and see what had set him off.

It was a cat. Of course. The black and grey tabby was perched on top of the back fence, its eyes locked with the dog's through the glass sliding door. The cat's fur was standing on end, its tail lashing back and forth like a cut snake. Kels could see its bared fangs as it hissed at the dog.

My God, the dog. He was throwing himself against the glass so hard the door was rattling in its pane, rearing up on his hind legs to stand as tall as she was, barking fit to wake the dead.

'Hey! Hey!' The dog ignored her. He hurled himself against the glass. There was a terrific crack. The next moment, sparkling shards were raining down, bouncing on the carpet. The dog went through the cascade in a black blur, seemingly oblivious to the hazard. The cat disappeared in a heartbeat, but the dog was after it - cast and all - up and over the fence while Kels stood there, stunned.

Oh fuck. Oh fuck.

'No!' she shouted and began to run.

Kels was reasonably fit, but not vaulting-over-garden-fences fit. She raced out onto the street. She could hear the dog barking, the sound getting further and further away from her. She pelted down the footpath in the direction of the ruckus, thinking: 'Oh God, oh God, my dog is going to kill that cat!'

She skidded around a corner and found herself across the road from the local church.

The cat had run up the old jacaranda tree standing in the corner of the churchyard. Kels could see it in the branches, hissing and spitting still.

The dog paced the footpath outside the churchyard. He looked mad, crazy, wild. White foam flecked his jaws. He kept rearing up on his hind legs – 'oh, shit his leg' - snapping at the cat. Thunderous growls and rumbles came from his chest as he fell back to pace and circle, back and forth along the churchyard fence.

'Dog! Dog!' Kels hurried up to him. She could swear there was a red gleam in his eye as he looked at her. His chilling growl reverberated down her spine, making her hand throb with remembered pain.

'Stop it!' She told him. She sounded hysterical, even in her own ears. 'Stop it right now! Sit!'

The dog didn't stop. The dog didn't sit. Out of the corner of her eye, Kels was aware of people gathering around, watching, silent. All of them were faceless. A gust of warm wind lifted her hair and wrapped it across her face. The smell of ozone hung heavy in the air. They would be in for a storm tonight. She reached for the dog with a trembling hand. He growled again, baring gleaming white teeth, but her hand closed on the soft leather of his collar without incident.

'Come on!' Kels was angry, and she was crying. 'Come on, you stupid animal!' She dragged at the dog. It was like trying to move a freight train.

'Come on!'

Slowly, step by step, they started moving towards home. The dog's growls faded, becoming more of a whine. He wanted the cat. Kels wasn't sympathetic. The wind rustling in the leaves of the trees that lined the path sounded like people whispering as they passed. Behind them, the church bell began to toll the hour.

Kels sniffed and wiped angrily at the tears on her face with the back of her bandaged hand.

'I ought to call you 'Trouble',' she muttered.

The dog made a chuffing sound deep in his chest.

She duct-taped an old sheet over the hole where the glass sliding door had been. It billowed in the wind that had kicked up, faint rumbles of thunder heralding the approaching storm. Kels didn't think that the sheet would do much to keep the rain out, but it was the best she could do given the circumstances. She thought about ringing Adam and asking him to come over and bring a proper tarp, but part of her was just too tired and heartsick to want to explain what had happened to him.

She was going to have to get rid of the dog.

The realization wracked her with guilt. She had only wanted to do the right thing. But she couldn't keep this animal. He was too big, too strong, too ….

… Scary.

And still, Kels felt guilty, because she knew what would happen if she took him to the RSPCA. He'd fail their tests. Be dubbed un-homeable.

End of the line.

But what was she supposed to do?

It was the thunder that shocked her awake. Kels had dozed off, curled up on the couch. The rain was really pouring outside, drumming on the roof. She was cold. She shivered, running her good hand over her arm, struggling to sit upright.

She had been dreaming. Echoes of the dream lingered in her head still - the world-shattering blast of a horn, the ferocious glare of headlights, and a heart-pounding sense of dread. A hot and stinking wind.

The dog. Where was the dog? Kels sat up fully and looked around. He wasn't in the lounge room. Unfolding herself stiffly from the couch, she went to look for him.

'Dog?' Kels called softly, stepping into the kitchen. It was pitch black. She reached for the switch - nothing.

'Shit,' she muttered.

She heard the click of his nails on the tile first. He was a ripple through the shadows, blending, merging with the darkness through which he moved. Except for his eyes. His eyes gleamed with a strange light - wild, feral - unnatural.

Clammy sweat broke across Kels' skin.

'Hey there, boy.' She found herself backing away. A terrible smell, like days old roadkill, swirled around the kitchen. Gorge rose in her throat. The dog was carrying something.

'Whatcha got there?' Kels tried to keep her tone light, friendly. It didn't work. Her voice was too high, too shrill. She stumbled back another step.

'Is that one of your toys?'

The dog dropped the whatever-it-was on the kitchen tiles.

It landed with a wet thwack. Outside, lightning cracked, and thunder boomed, and in the flash of light that came through the kitchen window Kels saw the dead cat clearly. Its grey fur was drenched and streaked with red, its green eyes lifeless, wide and staring. Its little mouth was open in a horrible scream.

Kels slapped her good hand across her mouth to stifle her squeal, her ass and then her shoulder slamming painfully into the doorframe as she jerked back. The dog barked, then growled, pacing forwards.

'No.' Hands scrabbling now, Kels found a grip on the doorframe, scrambled backwards with her back against the wall, down the hallway, tripping on her own feet. The dog followed, slowly, deliberately, head down, ears back, teeth bared.

'No, no, no, no.' Her heart was pounding. 'No! Go *away.*'

The dog growled again. It was an ancient sound, a primal sound, that melted Kels' bones and turned her lungs to splinters. She whimpered in response. The dog's eyes were no longer yellow. They were red - as red as the deepest heart of a flame; as red as the blood of the cat still dripping from its jaws.

Far too frightened now to scream, Kels turned her back on the dog and ran.

The air behind her shattered apart with the dog's barrage of barking. She bolted for the bathroom - the only interior door with a lock. Her eyes were blurred with tears. She was only strides away from safety when the dog slammed into her. Kels heard the screaming truck horn ringing in her ears; felt something very like a truck smash her legs from under her; heard the ferocious snarl and felt the explosion of pain. Time failed to slow. If anything, it speeded up, everything a whirl of dark and pain and an actual blinding flash as her head ploughed straight into the doorframe on her way down. Her shoulder followed suit. Teeth and fangs were tearing at her flesh, her back, her thighs, and she found the breath to scream - a high, thin sound. She kicked and squirmed, lashed out with elbows and fists - managed to half-turn, and get bitten on the arm. Kicking blind, Kels was rewarded with a yelp, and, surging with adrenaline, slithered and scrambled forward on all fours into the bathroom, where she tried to slam the door.

The beast's hellish head thrust into the room, growling and snarling. Kels slammed the door against it, heard it shriek in pain and rage. She shoved against the door with all her might, pushing against it with her feet, as the dog pushed back from the other side, like a hideous parody tug-o-war. The door snapped and strained under the pressure, long splinters of wood breaking free. Lighting cracked outside, flashing through the window like a black and silver strobe light.

With a final, gruesome crunch, the bottom half of the door gave way.

*

Trev Jones was on his way home from work. It'd been a long shift. He drove on autopilot, with his mind on the six pack of Hahn Superdry waiting cold in the fridge, and whether or not he should swing by Maccas or order a pizza once he got home. Overhead, good old Mother Nature was putting on quite the lights show. Trev was jerked from his mental debate between Big Mac or Loaded Meat Lovers by a massive prong of lightning, which speared down from the sky to strike the road in front of him.

'Woah, shit!' Trev cried. 'Awesome.'

The radio, which had been blasting Meatloaf's Bat Out Of Hell, fizzed and popped. Trev glanced at it, leaned over to give it a good thump with his fist. The static just got louder, so shrill that it made Trev wince. For the barest of moments, he closed his eyes, turned his face away from the road and into his shoulder.

When he looked up again, it was to see the flash of yellow eyes in his headlights.

He didn't even have time to hit the brakes. Trev felt the impact as he hit the - whatever it was – and heard a distinctly canine squeal as the car bumped over a solid object in the road. He slammed his foot down on the brake so hard that his four-wheel-drive started to fish-tail on the wet asphalt, tyres shrieking protest.

Trev's car finally stopped at an angle across the lane. He threw open his door, tumbling out into the road - and spotted the dark, furry heap lying in the darkness.

'No. Oh, no, no, no, no.' Trev ran to the dog, and slid down on his knees beside it. It was alive, whimpering and shivering. When Trev ran his hands over the dog's head in a soothing pat his palms came away slick with blood.

'It's okay, boy. It's okay. I'm gonna get you some help.' Trev reached under the dog, managed to lift it to his chest, then raise himself to his feet, grunting with effort. It had to be one of the biggest bloody dogs Trev had ever seen - maybe even some sort of part-wolf, he thought. It weighed a fucking tonne. Staggering, Trev carried the crying dog to his car, settled it as gently as he could into the back seat. Clambering in himself, he fished his phone out of the centre console and dialled the vet who treated his kelpie, Scoob.

'Hello? Jim? Mate, it's Trev Jones - yeah, that's right, Scooby's Dad. Listen, I've just hit a dog on the road. I think it's hurt bad. Can I bring it in?'

He listened for a moment.

'Yeah? Okay, thanks. I'm on my way now.'

He hung up the phone, put the car into gear, and started driving. Trev glanced at the dog in the rear-view mirror. Its amber eyes met his.

'Jeez, you really came outta nowhere mate. Don't worry, though. Jim'll take care of ya. We'll see ya right.'

Overhead, lightning flashed again, and the following thunder sounded like a long, echoing growl.

Oaths Sworn
On Knucklebones

by
Nicole Rain Sellers

The Northern Lights flickered late this winter. Vör glanced up again at the greens and violets reflected from the armour of Freya's Valkyries. Then she turned toward the sea.

The single-masted longboat had been built by her young brother, and its only ornament was a carved boar's head with great tusks that jutted from the prow. Vör's companions waited under an oilskin shelter at the rear, Boljá, a wiry figure slung head-to-toe with weapons, his faithful bird Valti, and somewhere among the furs, Kenaz and Ask, Vör's twin polecats. They were all she had left in the world, and they were more than enough.

She hauled the ropes loose and leapt in at the bow. "We sail!" she shouted, her breath pluming white in the air.

*

Torrential rain fell as equinox neared. Vör and Boljá languished for days under awnings, bemoaning their exile and divining their future by the runes. Despite the cramped quarters and his one blind eye, Boljá looked away whenever Vör dressed, prayed, or made her ablutions. Resourceful as always, he pulled a stream

95

of oddments from his pockets – walnuts, whalebone needles, strips of dried deer meat, tiny green lemons, a set of musk-ox knucklebones fashioned into dice, and cakes of seal fat he used to kindle cooking fires.

The lyrebird Valti perched on Boljá's shoulder day and night, her crown feathers bobbing and her long tail veiling his ropy blond braids. Watching the two of them chatter reminded Vör of Odin, who was also blind in one eye, and wore a glossy raven on each broad shoulder. But Valti spoke far more subtly than a raven, in a dazzling array of voices. She squeaked like a polecat, thrummed like the beat of rain on oilskins, and mimicked their curse-words with a comical stridence.

"Cold and homeless again, my friend," Vör sighed, bailing water from the boat's gully in a tin mug. Her brother had known his craft even as an apprentice, and there were no leaks in this hull. Still, incessant rain gathered underfoot.

"So we are. But we've plenty to drink." Boljá winked his cloudy eye, took a swallow from his flask, and passed it over to her.

The fiery glogg did little to warm her heart. "Freya would never have released us. Nor Odin. They would keep me divining for water on their battlefields, reading balefire omens, serving Freya's every petty whim. Escape was the only way." She passed the flask back and spat over the side of the boat. "Freya demands all, and gives nothing."

"She gave you that." He pointed at the horned battle helmet of hammered bronze she wore over her close-cropped hair.

"This I earned," she said. "And I intend to use it."

"I intend to use it," echoed Valti.

"I've no doubt you will," said Boljá, ignoring the bird and

stretching his legs out on the rocking deck. "The two of us make unlikely allies, do we not? Attendant of gods and indentured thief." He touched the Yggdrasil tree tattoo inside his forearm. It matched Vör's exactly – victory marks from a fruitful raid last year. "We've seen much, survived much. And so we shall again."

He raised his flask and began to bellow a drinking song. Valti copied his cracked notes as if they were the sweetest ever composed, punctuating his pauses with squawks of "Skaal!" Vör lay back and closed her eyes with a chuckle. Kenaz and Ask slid around her, warm as scarves, and she dozed.

*

The rain slowed to a drizzle.

Vör sat cleaning her dagger with a scrap of oiled rabbit skin. With the seax's keen edge she triple-notched gull feathers and split a bundle of elm branches into flexible rods. Then she fletched each rod with a thin tail of feathers and whittled the tips to a point. A wary Valti watched on.

"Rest easy. Lyrebird feathers are useless for arrows," Vör smiled.

As she worked, her blue eyes measured the trajectories of sea birds zagging in the clearing sky. She confirmed the signs by finding her pouch of runes and fishing one out.

"We turn south for the spring," she told Boljá. He grunted his agreement.

*

Dripping tunics, a pair of hose and a velvet cloak sagged from a makeshift clothesline between the sail ropes and the prow's boar tusks. Boljá made a fire in the brazier to set below the drying clothes, while Valti pecked at a fish carcass he'd laid on a bench for her.

He watched Vör pace the deck, twelve angry strides each way. She twisted her spear in her hands, and jabbed it in the air with each pivot.

"Still stewing over Freya?"

"She bestowed on me this Valkyrie helm. Swore to train me to choose the bravest souls for Valhalla, to share her battle glories with me. Swore it! She agreed to free you when you'd worked off your pilferings. Liar!" She thrust the spear. "Five long years, enslaved as runecaster and stablehand. Housed in the storerooms and fed in the kitchens as though we were nothing!"

"Stop your squalling, girl. Freya's behind us, and good riddance to her. Come. Sit." Boljá patted the bench beside him. "This will cheer you." He produced six apricots from a deep pocket.

She sat, put down her spear and ate one marvellous rosy fruit, then another.

"And this too will cheer you." He pulled out two hessian purses secured with twine, set one in her hand and watched her untie it. Her eyes widened at the gold coins inside. "Freya and Odin hoard mountains of gold. They won't miss this. Though they might miss the guard I killed to get it," he admitted.

Vör recalled the Northern Lights' flare on the day they departed, and her nerves pricked. She rose to fill a tankard from the barrel and gulped at the glogg. This time it eased her mind.

Long into the night, lit by a moon nearing full, they drank

and played at knucklebones, recklessly wagering gold coins and winning them back just as easily. Before dawn they reclined side by side on the bare deck, hands behind their heads. Valti pranced on Boljá's chest while the waves clunked and slapped below. They scanned constellations that had been obscured for days by rainclouds, and mapped out their route by the wolf star and her cubs.

Boljá gloated over his recent raid. How slyly he'd he cut the throat of Odin's best guard, how sweetly he'd coaxed from the stables the mighty stallion that sped them to the harbour, how deftly he'd snatched those fat purses of gold from under the pillows of sleeping gods!

"Now here we lay at sea, with my bronze helm and your talking bird," Vör said, "for all the world like ragged versions of Freya and Odin themselves." Amused by the thought, she adopted Freya's fatuous tone. "Odin, please stop breaking wind. You will surely cause a hurricane."

"Woman, you have poisoned my dinner," boomed Boljá, playing along. "But I, great, all-seeing Odin, am ever silent on the subject of my wife's treachery."

"Oh!" Vör fluttered her lashes. "Do you dare question me? I, best of all wives and warriors? I of the golden tresses, and the golden tears, and the golden chastity belt?"

"Chastity belt, my divine arse! Thor's best lock can't secure that thing! What say you, ravens?" Boljá inclined his ear toward Valti. "Freya may do whatsoever she pleases, whensoever she pleases? Well of course! That is understood, and besides, I have other matters to deal with." His hands groped the boards around him. "Now where is my drinking-horn? And my best guard? And my purses of gold?" He cast about drunkenly, and they hooted with laughter.

Vör sat up, suddenly sober. "All time will end before I forgive her. I hate oath breakers above all else."

He propped himself on one elbow and drained the last of his glogg. "I know it well. And that is why I trust you, girl!" He slapped her hard on the back.

Daybreak tinged the eastern sky. Boljá stood, scratched his pale beard, and turned his good eye to survey the horizon. In the voice he reserved for his enemies, so gruff it was almost a whisper, he spoke one word, "Valkyries."

Vör jumped to her feet. A vessel of polished wood slid toward theirs, its sails bearing Freya's crest, a cat-drawn carriage emblazoned in gold on a purple background. Four identical vessels fanned out behind the first. Their towering larch prows curled back on themselves, and on each prow a figurehead loomed – a snarling cat with a fish's tail.

Vör's blood pounded. Freya had failed to recognise her finest Valkyrie, had instead subjugated her, and Vör would avenge the betrayal. Five years of rage tore out of her gut in a murderous scream. Jeers and ululations echoed back across the waves. Bracing one foot on the rail, crimson cloak billowing, Vör brandished her broadsword in one hand and her spear in the other. She sneered at Freya's army, knowing her shining helm would be unmistakable as one of their own, and the blasphemy would enrage them.

The longboat was small, but it was agile. They swung the sail and strapped it hard, and struck a bold north-westerly course through the widest gap between Freya's ships. Still the first vessel gained on them. Vör's fingers stroked the rough haft of her spear in anticipation of the coming chaos.

*

And as sure as day follows night, chaos came, with the thud of bone and the clang of iron and the whistle and sear of flaming arrows. The first Valkyries scrambled through the air from their high deck, limbs outstretched, plunging into the longboat like roaring birds of prey. Vör and Boljá skewered them through with their swords, shoving the slumped bodies overboard before they'd yet fallen.

Vör killed many Valkyries that day. Some she recognised, without fondness. With her barbed spear poised at her shoulder she dodged their blows, springing back to take aim again and again. She embedded her spearhead in enemy flesh with a shriek, the hard hate in her belly driving every blow. She set her boot on her victims and wrenched the spear out with equal viciousness, then turned for the next Valkyrie.

Boljá's axe flew about him in a semicircular blur. His arms arced, his feet curved left and right, and his sightless eye did nothing to reduce his precision. At times the axe left his hand, only to swing back to his sure grip after lopping off a limb or slicing the war cry from a Valkyrie throat.

Valti ducked and hovered, never straying far from Boljá's shoulder. When arrows set an awning alight, her sharp beak untethered one end and floated it at starboard, quenching the fire.

A brisk easterly wind took the longboat through and beyond

the enemy flotilla. In the next few hours they gained headway, forcing the heavy warships to reposition behind them. They could still hear faint shouts and the whizz of steel-tipped darts in pursuit, but the Valkyrie warriors lagged at a distance arrows could not broach.

By late afternoon the wind was ferocious. They had outsailed all but one enemy ship, and despite their manoeuvres could not prevent it drawing alongside them. The Valkyrie crew was diminished, but those left on board tried a new tactic by dropping a boathook into the longboat. Vör and Boljá were immobilised beside the larger vessel, and tumultuous waves tossed them like butter in a churn.

They tripped across the pitching deck to dislodge the boathook, and barrels, furs and braziers skidded with them. Kenaz and Ask wound their long bodies around the mast, then dove into knotholes to cling to sturdier struts beneath the boards. A stack of new arrows, a box of dried fish, tankards and Vör's treasured rune pouch bounced into the sea.

"My runes!" Vör stretched precariously over the rail to retrieve the pouch from the wash between the colliding vessels. It was the eve of equinox, the sacred blót of Ostara, and to lose the tools of her livelihood now was surely a bad omen.

"You don't need them." Boljá caught her with one hand, his legs locked around a bench, and held her back till she calmed. She protested, but the runes sank and were gone.

With one more stride Vör reached the boathook, and struggled to budge it. Along its rope a Valkyrie slid, descending backward. Boljá steadied Vör against the lurching while she levelled her bow and made her shot. Her arrow pierced the invader's thigh.

He spasmed and swivelled to the rope's underside where he hung in mid-air, lame leg flapping his cloak like a bat's wing. Vör's second arrow lodged in his neck. He let go the rope, gurgling a fountain of blood, and followed her runes into the sea.

Boljá's grin flashed in the fading dusk as he pointed up along the rope. She nodded and they climbed, smooth as snakes, to the warship. The two of them jumped onto the burnished deck unnoticed, and quickly dispatched four Valkyries at the oars. They stripped a bronze scabbard and a crossbow complete with quarrels from the bodies, and proceeded below deck, where Boljà filled his flask with potent Valkyrie glogg and stuck a jaunty red quill in one of his braids.

They followed the sound of voices to the dining hall, and with efficient sword strokes stopped the hearts of nine unarmed Valkyries seated at their dinner. Then they raided the larder, where round cheeses in wax, a whole leg of mutton, and three fresh loaves vanished into Boljàs cloak, and Vör acquired two excellent knives of shining steel.

Satisfied they'd killed everyone on board, they emerged back on deck.

"What now?" Boljà resembled a mongrel dog as he tore off mouthfuls of mutton. "We take this ship and leave the longboat?"

"No," said Vör. "My brother built that longboat. And I want nothing of theirs. We burn it."

Boljá's axe was in his hand at the clang of metal and the flurry of pumping wings. A lone Valkyrie stood in shadow behind a pile of crates. She'd unveiled a cage and thrown it open, freeing scores of ravens. They rose like a storm cloud dispersing, winged warnings to Freya and Odin, a message the gods would heed and answer without fail. The Valkyrie cackled her victory even as Boljá cut her life short.

Blood-soaked, weary and discouraged, they lugged a vat of tallow from the galley and dumped it across the deck. Straddling the polished rail before descending the rope, they shot lit arrows into every surface and sail, and set the warship ablaze.

Down in the longboat, legs bowed and forehead furrowed, Boljá heaved the boathook into the water. They raised the sail and let the wind take them, and the flames and smoke of the Valkyrie vessel receded in the distance.

*

The equinox moon glowed like a hen's egg in a nest of raven feathers. Vör sat awake by the ritual fire long after Boljá slept, holding her polecats to ease her worry. The last Valkyrie's cry for help would by now have reached Odin, and tomorrow Freya's army would increase tenfold. Only fate, the unknowable mystery of Wyrd, could deliver them safe to the new life they'd risked everything for.

Keeping the Ostara blót required pouring a sacramental draught over a stone altar, but they'd drained the whole barrel of glogg, and the only stones on board had been her runes. Improvising, Vör began the ceremony by piling Boljá's knucklebones in a heap and blessing them with rainwater from the drinking pail, but she balked at singing the invocation. What god of Asgard could she invoke? None would answer. The chief gods Freya and Odin had doomed her, and it was they who hunted her down.

Her sky-blue eyes searched the stars. In childhood she'd heard stories of an older god, one from the frozen Northlands who fought valiantly with bow and axe while skiing through knee-deep snow. God of oaths, god of rings, god of the ancient covenant of the winter hunt. She remembered his name and whispered it thrice.

"Ullr!" she called out loud. "We are at war with Freya and Odin. Pray fight this battle with us now at Ostara, or else speed us to Valhalla where we may settle our grudge."

In the silence, the waves surrounding the longboat began to rush and crest in white peaks. Vör squinted. A man's silhouette was appearing in the spray, materialising out of a blizzard of stars and seafoam, skating down the snowy slopes of night to meet her.

A huge silver wolfskin draped his head and shoulders, crowning him with pointed ears that twitched as though alive. His eyes shone sapphire as the night he'd emerged from, and he carried three of the largest bows she'd ever seen, strung with gleaming gut. The yew shield that flanked him was inlaid with black iron holly boughs, and carved with a great tusked boar like the one on the prow of her boat.

Vör felt Wyrd opening, and heard the voice of fate.

"Who dares to call me away from my yew grove, into the open sea?"

She observed him in the firelight. Icicles formed shimmering points in his dark beard and quivered in the fur cuffs of his sleeves. His spiral-toed boots were of reindeer hide, bound to the thigh with leather cords, and a pair of flat snowshoes dangled at his belt. The sharp smell of pine sap was about him, and also a crystalline sound, the sound starlight might make in pristine air, or fir needles swaying under snow.

She knelt and steadied her voice. "I am Vör, exiled runecaster of Odin, betrayed handmaid of Freya, forsaken of the Valkyries. Death snaps at our heels and there's no time left. Ullr, older and wiser than the gods of Asgard, I will pledge you my lifelong loyalty if you fight with us."

*

At the moment of equinox the sun flashed between the bronze horns of Vör's helm, then rose bright as the goddess Ostara over the sea. As they'd expected, Valkyrie ships surrounded the longboat in every direction, and showers of fiery arrows already issued from them.

Vör and Boljá watched Ullr summon power to his yew shield by circling his hands around it. Convex side upright it levitated, spinning above the longboat with an intense gonging. They planted their feet wide for balance as the shield's oscillation threw loose its iron inlays. Propelled at great speed, the metal projectiles met the hulls and sails of the Valkyrie ships, wreaking destruction. Dozens of Valkyries were struck and fell from their blasted ships.

When the shield returned to Ullr's hands it staved off all assault. He armed Vör and Boljá with yew bows light for their girth. He circled his hands around their quivers, and though they saw no change in their arrows, once knocked in Ullr's bows none could miss its target. They set to work felling every Valkyrie they set their eyes on.

The longboat was stationary, but an otherworldly gale howling from its sides repelled the enemy and held their approach at bay.

Meanwhile Ullr's arrows set even the farthest vessels alight, and many crews abandoned ship, choosing death by drowning over burning.

Against the gale a handful of strong Valkyries pressed close in a faering row boat. Boljà threw his axe to decapitate each man in turn, the axe looping back to his hand like a roosting messenger bird. He severed the last helmed head with a sickening crunch, and it rolled into the waves, leaving six headless bodies to drift back to their ship.

The waters around the faering swirled with blood and bobbing bronze helms, and from those depths came a monstrous, hairy head. Its gilt Valkyrie horns were a hundred times larger than those of the slain men. White eyelid membranes blinked across the giant, slitted pupils of its yellow eyes. Rivers gushed through its jagged teeth and between whiskers like rows of whale ribs. Below the beast's cat head, the thick body of a serpent undulated through the water, and five long amphibious tails wove up and down around the longboat.

A honeyed voice flowed from its menacing maw. "Now hear the words of Freya, wife of Odin and queen of Valkyries." It submerged, thrashing, then resurfaced, waterfalls sluicing from fur and scales. "I do not come to trouble you, god of old," Freya cooed to Ullr through the creature. "I come for the blind one. The thief. The Odin imposter." It twisted and hissed, then flipped a tentacle overhead, grasped Boljá and pulled him overboard.

Boljá's braids flew about his head as the monster reeled him through the air. His right hand drew his broadsword and swung it side to side, but it struck nothing. His left arm, axe and bow were engulfed by the strangling tentacle, and the seax strapped to his thigh was out of his reach. The tentacle plunged him down toward the water. Recognising his fate, Boljà stilled and puffed out his chest, holding his sword aloft.

With a squawk of dismay Valti darted for her master. The cat-creature smacked its lips at the sight of the lyrebird, but Valti escaped a juddering tentacle and passed close enough to Boljà to stroke his beard with her feathers. He muttered to her, and after one last pass she flew to the longboat and alighted on Vör's shoulder.

The monster submerged Boljá until only his stalwart face and sword were visible. Tears coursed down Vör's cheeks, but she raised her chin and her sword in salute, and cried out, "Warrior! I will meet you in Valhalla!"

Freya's beast purred at Vör, "You too shall pay for your treachery, slave." It slapped a tentacle at her, a cat batting a mouse, but stopped short with a hiss as its yellow eyes met Ullr's sapphire glare. Teeth gnashing, it dove under Boljà's legs and bit him in half at the waist. His blood flowered in the water, and the sea monster sank into the red bloom, apparently satiated.

Vör swayed like a tree under an axe, broken, heartsick, every part of her bruised. An arrow protruded from her shoulder, and blood streamed down her back and trailed along one arm to drip from her fingers.

She watched Freya's bloodthirsty emissary weave its way northward, tentacles glinting in the water, a pair of listing Valkyrie ships following behind. A shrill ululation and the palest ripple of Northern Lights faded on the horizon. Why should she survive? She doubted Freya had spared her life to atone for past offences – more likely she'd found Ullr too powerful to challenge.

Ullr lifted Vör upright and laid his hands on her back. The arrow slid out of her shoulder, and in a single instant she felt her wounds knit and her bruises heal. The air around them surged and shimmered with vitality. When she turned and clung to him the skin of his arms was cool, but lightning pulsed underneath.

Raw with the tragedy of loss and flooded with the thrill of battle, she swept Valti and the polecats aside and pulled Ullr into the sleeping-furs.

*

Even in daylight, onyx stars sparked in the aura that rose all about him. When he shrugged off his wolfskin, bright crocuses fell out of his garments like comets from night. The dusky surface of his skin glittered with what appeared to be millions of snowflakes.

At his throat, wrists, and ankles he bore silver torque tattoos etched as wreaths of ivy, and to Vör's astonishment, each pointed ivy leaf furled and unfurled in constant motion. When she inhaled, his icy breath seared her lungs, and his sapphire eyes pierced hers like blades. The closer he pressed the more his chill burned, until she felt herself frosted to him, teetering skyward on a mountain peak.

"It may be beyond my station to bed a god," she gasped between kisses.

He shook his head, and minks roiled in the fjord of his hair. "Not so, runecaster," he said, removing her helm. "Gods have great need of the mortals who call them."

*

Vör's sleepy finger stirred the pools in Ullr's hair and traced the thunderbolts under his skin. While she'd never feel cold travelling with him, the Southlands she sought would be far too warm for this god of winter.

To find a new destination, she cast the knucklebones.

"Bones of the northern musk-ox," he said. "As fit for augury as for ritual. Tell me, what do you see?"

She pointed at the path of afternoon sun on the waves. "I see us head west, to the green isle I've heard tales of. There I see us prosper in the ways of the old gods. But first, we seal our agreement."

She pressed the tip of her seax into her palm, and a scarlet droplet rose there.

"Once seekers in stone circles offered me rings of iron. But rings are for those with human fingers and human limits. It was not their rings I wanted, but their oaths." He extended his palm, and when she pricked it an iridescent indigo bead appeared. She placed her hand in his.

The silver ivy tattooed at his wrist curled and sprouted tendrils, its leaves leaping their clasped hands to twine up her arm to the shoulder. Surprised, she released his grip, but the vine remained marked on her skin.

His eyebrows lifted. "You have sworn a vow. It is binding."

She smiled and took his other hand.

He ran cool fingers over the Yggdrasil tattoo inside her forearm, and its blue roots and branches widened, tangling across his own arm until every line of the tree was duplicated on his skin.

"Odin grew wise at Yggdrasil," he said, "and there he found

the sacred runes. But before Odin's time, Yggdrasil gave its wisdom to me, and to gods far older."

"Gods now forgotten."

He nodded. "I have languished too long in the north. I shall plant a grove of yews on your green isle, and watch them grow mighty as Yggdrasil. And in exchange I will give you an oath."

Her eyelashes froze, branches framing blue sky.

"I vow loyalty for your lifetime, and when you go meet your kin in Valhalla, I will remember your name to our children's children's children, as you remembered mine."

Kenaz wrapped Vör's elbow in a warm fur loop, and Ask ringed himself softly round her neck. Her eyes met Ullr's, sky and sapphire, mortal and immortal. It was enough.

"Let it be so," she said.

"Let it be so," agreed Valti, jostling the polecats for her perch on Vör's shoulder.

Vör handed Ullr the knucklebones that had served her as dice, altar and runes. His hands closed around them, reopening to reveal luminous yew seeds. These he secreted in a deep pocket under his wolfskin. Vör smiled, thinking of Boljá.

"Plant them well," she said.

His arms encircled her, and she inhaled the resin of pines, and the hum of stars, and the chill of snowstorms. She looked across the waves to the western horizon, where an emerald green isle lay sleeping in blankets of mist.

Prophesy

by
Dan Robb

"It's my turn!"

"Nah! You already moved. I seen you."

"I saw you," Sarah corrected reflexively.

"What do you know," Thomas snapped. "You're not Mrs Keel."

"I still know more than you do, cloud brains." Sarah lunged at the dice. Thomas followed and the debate quickly descended into a grappling match on the floor.

"What is it now you two?" Sarah and Thomas froze — fists full of hair, ribs full of knees — and turned to see their mother stepping delicately down the stairs to the living room. She was a tall woman, always immaculate and always frowning. A log smouldered in the fire place filling the room with a warm glow and the smell of a winter afternoon on a thick rug. "It never ends with the pair of you," she said. "I tell you I thought twins would get along better."

Thomas took his foot off his sister's throat and in turn Sarah withdrew her teeth from his arm. They stood and gave their usual parody of remorse. "Sorry mother."

It was then that Thomas noticed the book their mother had been reading. "What's that?" It was red with silver bits on the corners and there was a funny symbol on the cover, like an hourglass but round at the top and bottom.

"It looks like a magic book," Sarah said.

"Magic books are bigger," Thomas said with scorn. "And they're called *tomes* dummy."

"That's enough." their mother snapped and the pair fell silent … for a moment.

"What is it?" they repeated in unison as soon as she had returned to her perusal.

"I don't know." The answer was truthful, earnest, and entirely unsatisfactory. "It belonged to your grandfather. That's about all I know. I thought it must have been important because he called your father into the hospital to talk about it at … the end. He wouldn't discuss it over the phone and I wasn't allowed in the room with them." She turned the book so that her children could see the blank pages within. "I don't see why. It's almost empty, apart from some half-finished stories at the front, and even they're not very good." She started flicking through the pages again and turned to leave.

The twins looked at each other. They weren't buying it. "Why haven't we heard about it before?" asked Sarah.

"What did father do with it?" Thomas prompted.

Their mother's eyes narrowed. She generally felt that she could trust her children as long as they weren't working together. Mrs Keel sometimes said that together the whole world wouldn't stand before them. They were something of an anomaly — a male/female pair of identical twins. Both with white blond curls, both with freckles, both with the palest blue eyes you would ever see. Sarah had her mother's height however, while Thomas was broader across the chest like …

"Your father," she began but her voice caught. She clenched her fists around the leather book and breathed to calm herself. "Your father's accident was the following day. He brought the book home and stuffed it in his chest. I didn't even … I didn't even get to say goodbye let alone ask about the stupid book."

"But what is it?"

Her face screwed up and she tossed the book onto the game board at her children's feet. "There. You make some sense of it."

Sarah and Thomas watched their mother flee the room and shrugged to each other. They regarded the red and silver book with awe, with wonder, and without a moment's thought for possible consequences.

"Half written stories," Thomas breathed.

"I bet I could write a whole one," Sarah said. She snatched the book off the ground.

"I want to write a story," Thomas complained. "One with a knight!" His eyes lit up and he rushed for their drawing supplies returning a moment later with an orange pencil.

"Orange?" Sarah demanded dropping the book so that she could thrust her fists onto her hips. "You don't write stories in orange!"

Thomas shrugged. "I couldn't find the others. What difference does it make?" He dove on the book, flipped it open and managed to scrawl: Once there is a Knight with a huge sword, before Sarah wrestled him away.

"I'm writing it!" she said. "Nobody deserves to have to read your handwriting. And it's about a witch."

"Pfft," Thomas snorted. "A witch. My knight would easily

beat your witch in a fight."

"No he wouldn't! My witch would turn him into a frog or something."

"She can't! That's not fair."

Sarah put hands on hips again.

"I mean, she can't because my knight has a magic shield that blocks magic spells."

"That doesn't even make sense. Anyway, my witch would still beat your knight."

"Oh yea? How?"

"She has … a gun!" Sarah said triumphantly.

"A gun?!"

"Yeah," she snatched the pencil from Thomas's disbelieving hand and wrote, and a witch with a gun! in a loopy hand with little smiley faces as punctuation.

"Fine." Thomas recovered and joined his sister on the floor. "What if they're working together to defeat an evil …" he gesticulated vaguely.

Sarah gave him a sideways look and sighed. "Bad guy?"

"Yeah, I guess so."

'An evil Bad Guy', Sarah wrote with a shake of her head. And then she brightened. "Oh, maybe he's an all-powerful sorcerer who can summon hordes of demons!"

"No no no. He's just a … a …"

"Bad Guy?"

"Well yeah. With an army."

"That's stupid. Why does he have to be a man anyway? Why not an evil woman?"

"Because he's a Bad Guy." Thomas frowned at his sister as if trying to figure out when she'd hit her head. "A Bad Guy, can't be a girl."

"So?" Sarah blinked. "Yes he can. Shut up Thomas." And then she scrambled over the top of the book, threw some things around, and returned with the dice from their game. "Let's settle this."

*

"It's my turn!"

"I'm still looking."

Sarbon cursed and tied the reigns of their mounts around a tree branch. "You said two minutes. I'm coming up."

Torma spun as quickly as she could without raising her body from the stony ridge. "No! They'll see us."

"From up here?" Sarbon crawled up the ridge and gave her a look that spoke long-suffering volumes.

Torma raised a hand to stop him but then just shook her head and turned back to the plain below.

It was alive like a kicked anthill. The shining steppes were a day and a half to ride from any one side to the other. And they were almost entirely covered by a grey armoured, black tented, and red bannered army. The sun set early in these mountains and visibility was already fading. The daily bustle of the military camp was giving way to the glow of campfires and the steady murmur of night.

"It doesn't matter how many times I see those banners," Sarbon said. "I'll never get used to them. They're ludicrous." Each was a giant t-shirt upon a tall pole, a sight that might have made an enemy laugh if it weren't for the blood. The t-shirts were stained and dripping with blood. Pessimists would tell you that it was goat's blood but Sarbon wasn't so sure. The Bad Guy's unification of the world had been a messy one.

"No more ludicrous than the rest of the world since the sowing," said Torma quietly.

"'The sowing of Chaos'," Sarbon sneered. "Don't tell me you're actually buying that nonsense from the old men."

"The prophets," Torma stressed. "Have guarded the tome since even before the Scions of Chaos corrupted it. Their line are the only ones who can use it. They're the only ones who have any chance of understanding and fixing," she gestured irritably at the world "this."

"They're a bunch of crazy old men." Then Sarbon's tone changed. "What are we going to do Tom?" he asked.

Torma sagged against the ground for a moment before pushing herself back from the ridge and standing. She had been enjoying the argument about the prophets. Even more than usual she realised. It had been a way to avoid their actual problem. She kicked at a stone. "There aren't many options left to us Sar."

Sarbon joined her by their mounts. "We have to get to the Black City before the equinox. The Black City is on the other side of that plain."

"But we can't ..."

"We don't have time to go around Tom. And the simple facts are that the shining steppes are in our way so we have to go through them; and the Bad Guy's army ..."

"The whole damn army," Torma grumbled, kicking another stone.

Sarbon spared just a moment to nod in agreement. "All of the Bad Guy's army, every one of his soldiers is on the steppes. So we have to go through them."

"But we can't Sar."

Sarbon didn't reply. He Hedrew the gun from his hip and studied it. Guns used to fire some kind of projectile as he understood it — he didn't know why, anything that came out of such a small hole would do little to a man in armour. Now they were used symbolically. They served a similar purpose in witchcraft to a jaw bone or burnt church wood. "I'm the most powerful practitioner in generations," he said quietly, "and I've been trained for this since I could babble. You and that sword of yours are more deadly than I ever will be. If anyone can cut a path through that army it's the two of us but ..."

"There are just too many."

The witch didn't reply. He absently kicked at a stone which skittered sideways startling his mount.

"Dammit Sar." As Sarbon's resolve flagged, Torma's bolstered — they couldn't both sulk like little girls. "This is why we were sent," she said. "Only we can get it there. This is why."

"There are too many of them for us to simply charge down there."

"What else can we do?"

Sarbon stopped and stared over the plains for a long while. In a cleft in the distant mountains there was a jagged shape like a blood darkened knife point. The Black City. He stared for a long time and Torma waited patiently. She knew the answer already but she knew that her friend needed to think it through. Finally he shook his head and swung into the saddle.

The heavily muscled witch kept that far-away look in his eyes as they mounted and rode to meet the Bad Guy's army on the shining steppes.

Stay with me, Torma thought. I need you with me.

The Bad Guy's soldiers were a hideous blending of human and reptile; not lizard or snake; something darker, fiercer. The lands that the Bad Guy plundered were scoured for men, farmers and kings alike and those who survived the change were turned into red scaled, yellow toothed monsters. Most wore ash grey armour and carried swords or pole arms. About one in a hundred was larger and leathery wings stretched from its shoulder blades; even more rarely there was a white one with red eyes. They were the ones who scared Torma the most. They were the spell casters.

When the enemy saw them the camps erupted. Torma screamed and raised her sword. Sarbon's battle cry joined hers. Their mounts, as one, lowered spiralled, white horns; their rainbow tails left twin ribbons of glitter behind them and the battle was joined.

As always, the clarity of thought before a fight shattered into a million red gleaming shards as the first blow was struck. As the first spray of hot blood coated Torma's face. As the first screams filled the air.

The knight roared death and hatred.

Red scaled and leather winged shapes flashed at her from the darkness and she cut them down. Her sword was the length of a man and a half, long enough to unseat a rider or cut down a flyer before it even got close, but light enough to swing one handed. With it, Torma painted death in all directions.

Sarbon pointed his gun left then right, above him and then

behind. Each jab of the strange weapon brought a burst of flame and a cry of death.

When one of the white scaled casters appeared sending a flaming black ball at the pair Sarbon reached out and stopped it. He swung the dark magic over his head like a lasso and hurled it back. The caster deflected it but was off balance when the ground opened up and swallowed it.

The defenders became denser as they reached further into the melee. And they encountered more and more flyers and casters.

Sarbon had stopped flinging the fireballs back at their casters. There were too many now. And Torma spent more time defending than she did attacking.

But still they fought.

Lightning struck all around them sending bodies into the air and Torma left a swath of corpses in their wake. But the press of defenders on all sides closed in.

The doubts that had plagued Sarbon as they rode for the plains had left him now. They had chosen their course and it was too late to rethink it. All there was left to do was fight, and keep fighting, and hope that it was enough. They had to get the book of prophesy to the Black City. For only there could what was written be un-written.

But they weren't going to make it.

"There!" Torma shouted.

Sarbon looked and saw it too. A t-shirt banner dripping blood. This one twice the size of any other and completely red-washed. The Bad Guy's personal banner.

They made for it, blasting and scything away defenders, but the Bad Guy's soldiers pushed back with redoubled zeal. A bronze palanquin had barely come into view before the press of bodies around them became too great.

The Bad Guy's personal guard surrounded them now. Sarbon surveyed the army, there was not a single foot soldier in sight. All around them were wings and white scales.

The knight and the witch drew rein side by side, watching each other's back. "One last push."

Dark shapes circled overhead and black flames grew in an unbroken circle around them. Torma gritted her teeth. She knew what was coming.

A roar from above triggered it. In an instant the Bad Guy's elite were diving and charging, black flames and long spears assailed them. Torma reacted and Sarbon was only a heartbeat behind.

He swept his gun in an arc towards a section of attackers and a wave of earth launched them back. He raised the gun to the sky and a hurricane answered his call.

And then he took a spear to the hip.

The long shaft drove him from his saddle. As he rolled to the trampled ground it splintered and tore him open. He screamed and his gun tumbled out of reach.

Torma, assailed from all sides, amassed a wall of scaled bodies around her but she was bleeding from a head wound, unhorsed, and limping on the left side.

Two black fireballs streaked towards her. "No!" Sarbon shouted and lunged forward, ignoring the pain in his hip, and grasped at his gun. Raising it, he aimed at the first of the fireballs and it swung into the sky. The other stayed true.

Torma turned and saw it. Her eyes widened. And she raised

her shield.

The magic never reached the golden shield. It burst. Black flames washed over and around the knight but they didn't touch her.

Sarbon scrambled to his knees and stared. Torma gave him a guilty smile before turning back to the fray.

"ENOUGH!"

Everything stopped. An unnatural quiet settled on the battlefield. The booming voice was like an earthquake given life.

Life? No, Torma corrected herself. There was no life in that voice. Just authority. Immense Power.

In the direction of the palanquin a knot of scaled warriors parted to let through a tall figure in black robes. "That's enough for now," the Bad Guy said mildly. He was tall and bony. His head was shaved. His eyes were … red, glowing like the coals at the bottom of an old fire. "You are mighty indeed," he said. "The prophets have chosen well. It would be a shame, I think, for you to die at the hands of such rabble." he gave them a smile that stretched his lips grotesquely over protruding teeth. "I think you've earnt yourselves a death by my personal hand. A rare honour."

Then he laughed. It was a sudden, violent thing that rolled away across the stormy sky. The Bad Guy held Torma's gaze while he laughed. And when he stopped it was abrupt and absolute, his face fell back to the grim blankness of before.

Torma turned to Sarbon and was pleased to see that it had creeped him out as much as her.

"But first, give me the book," the Bad Guy said.

"Never," Torma said. She found herself the spokesperson in

these situations. Sarbon could prattle all day when it was just the two of them but he let her do the important talking. He would think of something annoyingly profound to say at the end.

"Look at all the trouble it's caused you, that little book. Look at the trouble it's caused the whole world. Not that I'm complaining, I owe quite a lot to that little book of orange scribble. Don't you feel duty bound to destroy it? To stop all of this happening again?"

Torma snorted. "I bet you'd like that. The book of prophesy isn't the problem. It was corrupted by the scions of chaos."

The bad guy laughed again at that. And then he stopped. "The Scions of Chaos. The much reviled and feared Scions. Do you want to know the truth of the Scions of Chaos?" He arched a long eyebrow in what might have almost maybe been amusement. "They were children. Just two bored children playing a game. And using that book they brought the world to its knees."

"Using this book the Prophets with bring you down." Torma tried to ignore the revelation. It didn't change anything. Still, her mind raced.

With words in the tome the Keepers of Prophesy shape the future as they must. "The Prophets can write a new future," she said. "They can finish your story and it will fade away just like so many before it. Under the light of the equinox they can even erase your story. They can erase you."

The Bad Guy raised his arms to the army surrounding them. The black winged flyers and the red eyed casters, thousands of them all around, shuffled eagerly. "Only if you get it to them."

Sarbon sagged against Torma for a moment. They were both exhausted.

"Before I end this let me offer one last time," The Bad Guy said and looked into Torma's eyes, a look that made her soul feel dirty. "Hand over the tome and serve me."

Sarbon straightened at that and raised his weapon. Muscles taut, and face grim, Torma thought that his response was a stroke of eloquent brilliance.

"No."

Lightning still struck randomly, the wind still buffeted those in the sky, and moans of anguish sounded from the dead and dying but within the circle around the Bad Guy it was all strangely muted. Torma reached into the pouch at her waist and touched the red leather book with the silver corners. The book of prophesy. The ruin of the world, and maybe its salvation. She raised her sword to point at the Bad Guy, mimicking Sarbon's pose.

Once there is a Knight, and a witch with a gun.

"No," they said together.

*

"It's my turn!"

Thomas rolled the dice. "Dragons!"

Sarah grimaced but dutifully wrote down, a massive army of dragon men. "And they were waving banners made out of?"

"Human faces," Thomas cried. He was quivering with excitement.

"You can't just say things," Sarah said for about the millionth time. "You have to roll the dice."

Thomas screwed up his face but he picked up the two dice

and rolled.

7.

Sarah selected a piece of paper with a seven at the top and twelve words listed beneath Thomas rolled again.

11.

Sarah paused. "T-shirt," she said flatly. Thomas stared at her. "Maybe there's something on the t-shirt banners. Roll again."

He rolled a 6, then a 1. Sarah took list number six and read out word number 1. "Blood."

"Now we're talking."

"So the witch and the knight …"

"With the magic shield."

"Yes Thomas. They ride towards the army on their horses."

"On their wolf mounts!"

Sarah gave her brother a withering look and he picked up the dice.

3 and 7.

"Unicorns!" Sarah squealed. "Yes. Oh yes yes yes." Ignoring Thomas's chagrin she scribbled: Riding their unicorns!

"So they kill all of the army and get to the Bad Guy …" Thomas started.

Sarah paused. "Should we rename him?"

"Nah. He's just going to die anyway."

"Says who?"

"He's the bad guy. He has to die at the end."

"No that's too simple." Sarah took on a lofty expression. "I think we are writing a tragedy Thomas."

Thomas frowned, frightened by the gleam in his sister's eyes. "What do you mean tragedy?"

"The heroes don't get to the Black City," Sarah said coldly. "They fail. The Bad Guy kills them."

"No way!"

"Yes way. Why do they need to get to the Black City anyway?" Sarah asked.

"I don't know" Thomas shrugged. He frowned at the question. "Should I roll the dice?"

"No," Sarah said. "I'm getting a bit tired of this to be honest. Shall we go outside?"

"Yeah OK."

"I'll just write that the Bad Guy won."

"No just say that they killed the Bad Guy!"

Sarah put her hands on her hips. "You're not the boss Thomas!"

"I'm older than you."

"No. I'm older than you!"

"I don't want the heroes to die."

"Well OK then. Roll the dice."

The Halo Effect

by
Nicole Rain Sellers

Fluoro dice spin up from the bottom of the screen, hundreds of them – ping, ping, ping – but no matches. The next guy's playing the same machine as me, Snake Eye Sensation. He's on a roll and his jackpot keeps trumpeting. As soon as he walks away I'm jumping on that one – mine's a dud. I'm down to my last twenty for fuck's sake.

To get rid of him I slap the button harder, yell abuse at my screen and slam my beer down on the laminated shelf between us, dousing his clothes. The guy jumps up, ready to have a go.

"Sorry mate, sorry mate." I open my arms like I meant no harm.

Duggo's on a machine across the aisle. That beefy bastard's had it in for me since the night me and Phoebe slashed his tyres – long story but he totally deserved it. Now Duggo sums up my ploy pretty accurately, which is a bit of a surprise for him. Not the sharpest tack in here, hey. He fronts up to me, eyes all shrivelled.

"You're a fuckwit, Owl."

"Piss off, Duggo." I'm checking out the credits on the other guy's screen while he's spluttering at me and lifting up his wet shirt.

Next thing you know Duggo's clobbered me in the back of the skull with a fucking barstool, and I'm crumbling in slow-mo like a brick wall under a sledgehammer.

I'm sprawled on the floor and I can, like, see myself from above, lying there with blood pooling under my ear, one arm stuck through the legs of the barstool, feet twisted sideways. Duggo the gorilla's just standing there mute, hands on his knees, staring down at me with his shrivelled-up eyes.

People start gathering round on the tiles. Even though I'm passed out I can see them all clear as day. Bunch of losers really. Three ordinary punters, Em the hooker, that lanky junkie Tim, a scrawny interstate truckie, four agro chicks wearing short skirts and fascinators from their Cup luncheon twelve hours ago, and the pungent Danish backpacker who lives upstairs.

"Oh my lord," breathes Stefan, the poncy perv who comes in weeknights on the hunt for new boys. He kneels, pulls out a hanky and dabs my forehead. I want to shake him off but I can't move or speak.

"Fuck off, Stefan. Give him some space," says Em. Em's cool – always did like her.

Maxine the barmaid appears over Stefan's shoulder, eyes all teary. "Poor Owl." She's been busy with her fortune-telling side-hustle, tipping winners in the TAB. "Duggo just bolted past me white as a sheet. I always knew he'd do something like this."

Heads swivel, but Duggo's long gone.

When Phoebe OD'ed I was so shattered I went home with Maxine one night. She's got this huge red bed draped in curtains and tassels and shit. She was keen but I was way too wasted to cooperate, and thank fuck for that – I never would've lived it down. That flashy dude who used to come in, fancied himself a gangster – what was his name again? He had a crack at Maxine on a dare and got laughed out of town for it. Just disappeared. Any brains he moved in with some girl too decent to recognise him for the lowlife he is. Or he went back inside, or some supplier he ripped off caught up with him. Who knows?

"I'm gonna be sick," grunts one of the fascinator chicks, and stumbles away, champagne glass still dangling in her talons. Her mates clipetty-clop off after her.

The middle-aged bouncer known only as Johnny Walker comes in last, probably hoping the drama clears itself up before he gets there. He looks at me unimpressed and calls it in on his radio. The guy I spilled my beer on's disappeared, and he was the only witness, but Johnny doesn't give a fuck, just slouches around in his usual zombie way till the cops arrive.

The ambos strap me up on a stretcher and carry me out. I can't believe how bright everything looks through my closed eyes. Red and blue lights strobe around the parking lot. They put me down outside the big peaked doorframe while they decide what to do with me.

Pine Inn, says the green neon sign. The Pineapple, we call it. So many times I've stood in this same spot, hey, to cool down, have a smoke, take someone on. Or watch the rain swirl in white bursts around the streetlights, like the stars in that painting by that French guy who cut off his own ear.

"Look, the halo effect!" Phoebe used to say when the drugs were good, or "Fuck. Another migraine," when they weren't. Either way she'd be glowing under the streetlights herself. The light and the rain would be bouncing off her, and that warm jasmine smell would be seeping out of her skin, radiating around us.

"Look at you. Phoebe the bright one," I'd say, and she'd give me that look, half pissed-off, half pleased, not caring about the mascara smeared down her face or the rip in her shirt from the scuffle she got in earlier. She'd stand there in the splintered light and my heart'd go to jelly – guaranteed.

And there it is now, the halo effect, right there above me. I'm coming to join you, Phoebes.

Two guys hoist me into the back of the van, get in with me and slam the door. The mask over my face tastes sour. It's not oxygen. A sedative maybe – good. The ambos keep yacking as if I'm not there. "Pine Inn… head injury… unresponsive… three-four-six," says a voice in the front seat, and we're away, sirens wailing.

Once I binge-watched the Matrix movies with my dealer Dave, and nicknamed him Neo. The name suits his buzz-cut and black eyes, so it stuck. That night we were tripped out on acid, laughing ourselves stupid at the double meanings in the movies, thinking they were meant just for us. We were at his place, stamping smiley faces on E tabs and bagging up weed. Every so often I'd go downstairs to scare off potential thugs lurking round the building. Neo always slips a little extra in my party packs to return the favour. He's a decent guy, and a good mate.

"So which will it be?" He wiggled his eyebrows. "The blue pill or the red pill?"

"Um, how about both?" I said, and we fixed up a powerball, my drug of choice. Risky but worth it. The opiate takes the edge off the amphetamine for a smoother ride without the crash. Unless you mix the shot wrong. I try not to think about that. And hey, I'm still here to tell the story, right?

I wish I was Morpheus and had all the answers. But in this matrix life people hate you, the world's cold and no one understands. Your more successful little brother rings now and then, offering to set you up in a day job. "Yeah, maybe next week," you say, but it never happens. The only thing you control is how you get high and who with. Anyway, you like the street people better than the straight people. So you stay.

It was Phoebe who introduced me to Neo. We were happy for a while, really happy. Then came the fights, and the clap, and the week-long benders. She had a temper coming down, and sometimes she'd smash things up, plates and shit, or scream in my face. Sometimes she'd slap me, even in public. I'd grab her enough to stop her flailing, but I never hit her back. It just wasn't in me – even on the worst days when we spat at each other like feral cats, slinking through trains, knocking off handbags, rolling creeps in their cars. Till we pulled the plunger on our next shot and the sun came out again.

Okay, so Phoebe was a bit damaged, but I'm not exactly a perfect specimen myself. And she was mine, more mine than anyone ever was, or ever will be again. I didn't ask about her past and she didn't ask about mine, but the things she did in the shower, and on the front stairs – she must've learned them somewhere, hey. That arsehole Hamish told me he saw her strip at the Royal once. I don't care if she did. It doesn't change anything.

Phoebe and me partied all night on whatever gear we could

afford, and curled up together all day, just talking shit if we couldn't sleep, lighting each other's smokes, rubbing each other's aches. Then one night I walked her to the station and she blew me a kiss from the train and I never saw her again.

Anyway, right now I'm laughing. The doctors've shot me full of adrenaline – maybe my heart stopped – and morphine – maybe I yelped in pain. Just jonesing probably, hey, but they don't know that. These chemicals fit in my blood like fucking keys in locks. I'm flying, for free.

My dopamine's singing sweet harmonies. My ribs sigh and swing open like Morpheus's ivory gates of oblivion. My veins are underground rivers of music, and my heart's a red cave full of poppies. And inside my heart-cave, bright Morpheus sleeps, dreaming up the future – the god Morpheus, the real one, not the one from the Matrix. My main man Morpheus has one ear like a bird-wing that hears everything, and get this – he grants every wish he hears.

On I nod, till I come around, shirtless, on a hospital trolley in a hallway. I pull my striped T-shirt back on and stroll right out of the ward. No one even notices, or tries to stop me.

I feel pretty fucking good – fit, nimble, pumped – and I'm strutting down the corridor, and I, like, leap in the air and click my heels, right and left. I break into a sprint and leap again, higher every time, till I'm running sideways along the walls, grinning ear to ear. All I need's an Uzi, a long coat and some dark shades, right? I'm fully into this Matrix scene.

I slalom right up the walls till I'm running on the ceiling, only I can't tell if the ceiling's up or down or what. And then the roof starts crumbling under my feet. Plaster splits off, bricks break and fall into a gaping black hole. Tiles hurtle out into the night sky.

Starlight pours from the hole into the corridor, turning it red like Morpheus's cave. The starlight pulls me up and out of the building, into the night, and then I'm fucking flying along in the breeze. I'm digging this whole thing by the way, and I know exactly where I'm going. So when I see the Pineapple there on the corner, I float down. Go in.

Everything's so bright – the streetlight halos, the lime-green sign, the fluoro pokies flashing. And it's raucous. I can hear every conversation, literally every word out of every mouth, and I realise I'm hearing it all through one ear, and my ear's feathered like a wing. Shit, I can even hear people's thoughts. But it's more than that. Just like Morpheus, I can hear people's dreams. I can see in their hearts. I know what they want.

No one at the bar notices me. I think I must be dreaming – or astro-travelling or whatever it's called, before I like, cross over to the other side. But then I hear, "Hey Owlie!"

My name's Owen, but they call me Owl because I last all night, on the ball for hours. And when the speed wears off – or the coke on a good night – and the smack kicks in, I perch on my corner barstool till closing, all wise and quiet, hoodie pulled up to hide my pupils. Or I don't know, maybe they just call me Owl because I've got round eyes and a pointy nose, hey.

Tim comes up and he's pale, jonesing for sure. "You look set, man. None around. Where'd you get it?" He shifts from foot to foot. "Thought you were in hospital. Hit me up?"

"You can see me?" I'm stunned, and if I'm honest, kind of disappointed.

"Yeah, ya fucken idiot, I can see you. Hear you too. Shit must be good, hey, makes you invisible and everything." The pool table lights sharpen his sneer and his collarbones. And I can hear his thoughts just as sharp. All he wants is a rush.

I gawk for a minute, trying to work this shit out. Maybe Tim's the only one here on my wavelength. Maybe that's why he sees me and no one else does. And that's when it hits me, what I'm meant to do.

"Tim, you've gotta take over now."

He frowns. "Whaddya mean?"

A chick in tight shorts jostles up to the bar. She's dreaming about lounging by the pool with a cocktail on a tropical cruise. "Talking to yourself again, Tim? You okay?" she says.

He nods, looking unsure.

"Don't talk," I tell him. "They don't know I'm here."

He rolls his eyes.

"Just listen," I say. "You're the man now, alright? I'm giving you my place, all my shit, and my stash."

That gets his attention, and now his eyes are big as saucers. I coach him on the best places to sell and how to be nice to my customers. When I give him the keys to my flat and tell him where the gear is, he grins like a meerkat, slaps me on the back and yells, "Mate, you're an absolute fucken legend!"

The chick in the shorts stops sipping her blue lagoon and turns around to shake her head at Tim.

"Sh," I remind him.

"Come back to my place? If you want," he suggests to the chick, who ignores him.

Offloading all my goods feels exhilarating. Can't take it with you, right? I leave Tim to it and go hit the dancefloor in the nightclub. The air con in there's packed it in again and it's hot, but You Shook Me All Night Long is playing loud enough to drown out my super-hearing for a while.

Everyone's sweating their guts out. Even I'm saturated, and I'm not even sure if I'm really here or just tripping out. Up the back, a few blokes and one butch bitch take off their shirts and hang them over wires connecting the humungous speakers, so I stick my shirt up there too.

Then I spot Duggo, guzzling Bundy-and-cokes and bouncing around in some fucked-up epileptic dance, on a mission to write himself off. He must've got bailed – or maybe the coppers never even picked him up – and snuck back in right under Johnny Walker's nose. After what he did to me I'd have to be a moron to pass up this golden opportunity.

I shoulder-tackle him – plough him right into the speaker wires and wet shirts. One of the speakers comes down and Duggo cops a nasty shock. Not enough to, like, electrocute him or anything, but there's a choice shower of sparks and a puff of smoke as he drops. It's fucking satisfying as. And no-one knows it was me, they just think he's slipped over shitfaced.

Duggo's heavy, but Johnny Walker drags him out, grumbling under his breath.

Somebody upstairs must be smiling on me, probably Phoebe hey, because Duggo's wallet falls out of his jeans as he slides across the dancefloor. I swipe it, pocket three hundred bucks – where the fuck'd he get that kind of cash? – and shove the rest in the overflowing bin in the Men's.

My mind ticks over then. I start to get creative. There's a race on at Dapto tomorrow, and my winged ear knows the names of the winning dogs – it's like hearing the wind whisper. I decide to give Maxine a big tip. Why not? I go into the TAB while she's over at the sports bar, and turn three of her tarot cards face up – the numbered ones, so they're spot-on for the trifecta. Let her think she predicted it.

Outside, I'm so into this good karma thing I swipe a rose from someone's yard, go down the road, jump in Maxine's window, and throw it right in the middle of her big red bed. She'll go apeshit trying to figure out who left it.

Next up is Neo's place. He's out, but I already know his wish – to be filthy rich. I fold the three hundred cash up in the sports pages and write on the outside in black marker, "Neo. Put this on Glad Rags in the fifth at Caulfield. It's all yours." I add a smiley face with big round eyes so he'll know it's me, and leave it on his greasy coffee table. I'm not sure how, but I know Glad Rags is going to win that race at twenty-five to one. With his business knack Neo'll turn the seven grand into seventy, fast. Then his next move's up to him.

I head back to the Pineapple. Em's working the lounge bar, bored shitless and hanging to go home. The stoner Danish backpacker's watching her while he slurps his schooner of ice water. He's fantasising about building their future kids a cob house on an avocado farm somewhere he can grow his own pot. Em doesn't give the love-struck sucker the time of day, so I lend him a hand by knocking his glass off the bar. When it smashes to the floor Em looks his way, and for the first she time really notices him.

It's like opening a window. I can see into their future, and that doesn't even surprise me now. They'll shack up in his room upstairs, no peep out of them for days apart from bistro phone-orders and the odd muffled giggle, and finally they'll come down holding backpacks and announce they're hitching up to Darwin to visit Em's mob. And they'll take off – just like that. About time the pair of them got together, hey. Been in this shithole long enough.

It's not hard to find Johnny Walker. He's in his usual spot, on the ledge under the green neon sign, staring into space. He can be a useless dickhead at times, nobody knows that better than me, but now I hear his private thoughts I see he's not a half bad bloke. Just needs a break, and hasn't had many in his life. Happens to be an Armguard dude at the bar tonight, so I elbow, nudge and push him all the way out the front. He lights up a smoke and he and Johnny get talking, and no shit, turns out Armaguard's hiring. He gives Johnny the number to call and goes back inside. Johnny's always wanted a gun license, and he sits there smiling to himself.

Sounds like the speakers are on again – the DJ's playing Wonderwall. The sun'll be up soon, it's like four AM, and the garbos roll by and empty the bins. I reckon my work's done. I just stand there breathing, and the halos on the streetlights breathe with me, pulsing in and out. Phoebe's calling.

I lift off the ground and float up towards the stars in slow spirals – a freaked-out, one-wing-eared, lopsided, wise owl, right on target back to my heart-cave of poppies. I'm thinking I'm about to astro-travel through Morpheus's golden gates of forgetfulness, and I'm stoked to go rest in Phoebe's arms where I belong. I look down one last time and I know I'll never see the

Pineapple again.

I'm like, catapulting through the stars, on and on. And then shit gets weird. I start coming down, spinning out. I see myself lying in a hospital bed, a proper one now, with a drip in my arm, one eye swollen shut, and a massive bandage on one side of my head. Fuck off, I think, did I lose an ear?

Morpheus from the Matrix waits in the corner with his dark shades on. The machine I'm strapped to hums waves of green code. My little brother's sitting at the foot of the bed in his work shirt and tie, looking worried, the sentimental bastard.

And Phoebe's there too, standing right next to me. She smells like jasmine on a warm night, and light's splintering all over her, swirling around her, pouring out of her across the bed.

"Time to join you, hey Phoebes," I smile.

"No," she says, hand on her hip. "Time to get clean."

The halo effect on her face and hands is distracting, and I'm thinking fuck, are those angel wings sprouting out of her shoulders? But then she points her finger at me and says, "And so help me, I will kick your arse again if you relapse. Don't make me do that, Owl."

Kick my arse, again? What the fuck? Was it Phoebe behind this whole fucked-up night? I look at Morpheus.

He nods, and now a rain of green matrix codes is pouring over me, blurring my vision, leaking out from under my eyelids. And I realise there's one more gate I've got to break through – Morpheus's final, iron gate of truth.

Morpheus comes over, takes off his shades and slides them onto me, one side stuck in the bandage. Then he disappears into thin air. I can't see shit now, but I know he's gone.

My brother's watching me. He notices a change and gets up. "Owen," he says. "Owen. You thirsty? You hungry?" I hear his hopes for my future, feel his hand on my arm. And yeah, I am hungry – for eggs, bacon, coffee. For health, for life. I'm ravenous, but I can't leave Phoebe yet. I'm dreading the tremors, the sweats, the itching, the spewing. I want to stay longer.

But Phoebe gives me that look, half pissed-off, half pleased, and she whispers in my good ear, "Don't worry, I'll be here," and I know this is what she truly wants. So when she says "You ready?" I nod yeah, ready.

I push open the iron gates leading out of my cave, and I step into the real world.

Only the world's different now. Everything's sharper, the colours are brighter, and what people want is clearer, even when they're not talking. The future's like an open window inviting me to look through it. I'm on a new wavelength, hey.

Two-Wheel Pony Express

by
Meg Smith

Coming down the last of the hills, Suki sat up straight in her saddle and let the bike coast beneath her. Despite the storm two nights before, the high sun had baked the mud dry and her wheels kicked up the dust. She kept an eye out on the road ahead, looking out for Margo. The other woman's heavily-laden bike was bigger, but it had an electric assist motor, so she always beat Suki to the top of the hills. When Suki finally caught up with her, Margo was stopped where the road met the edge of the river.

'Shit,' Suki said, pulling up alongside.

'Yep,' Margo replied. 'This is bit of a problem.'

The rain had flooded the river. All that was left where the bridge should have been were a few posts in the middle of the rushing water and some broken timber struts swinging lazily on the other side. The rest had been completely washed away.

Margo looked up from under sweaty brown curls. 'Is it the start of the Wet, do you reckon?'

Suki bit her lip and looked at the water again. It had clearly come down hard up river, but the water was receding.

Suki shook her head. 'No, I don't think so. Just an early storm. Still, it might as well be if there's no bridge to cross.'

Margo rested her elbows on her handlebars, her chin in her

hands and looked at Suki. The bulky cargo bike looked far too big for her, but she handled its unwieldy weight with comfortable ease born of familiarity. She shrugged. 'There are other ways across the river.'

For one brief moment, Suki thought Margo was suggesting they swim, dragging their bikes across. But then Margo continued: 'There's Mungo's Crossing south from here.'

Sui nodded. 'The ferry there makes several crossings a day.' She hesitated.

'But…?' Margo prompted.

'But it's two days ride from here, plus two more to get us back to the route.'

'Ugh, that's cutting it fine.' Margo frowned at the river. 'Those early storms have got me worried we're in for an early Wet.

They were headed for New Garden, an outback farming community in mid-western New South Wales. The payload they currently carried between them was a little over 120 kilos of essentials, not the least of which being seed, which the community would need before the next planting. Which they wouldn't be able to deliver if the Wet washed out the roads before they could even get there.

'There's Blacksmith's Bridge to the North,' Margo said squinting upriver. 'That's only one day's ride from here. Less, if we push it. If we can up the pace on the other side, we'd still make it to New Garden before the Wet with a little luck.'

Suki looked at the fast rushing water below them and the jagged remains of the bridge. 'What if Blacksmith's is washed out too? Then we'll still have to turn around and head to the ferry. Except then we'll be four days behind before we even get across.' She shook her head, 'It's too risky.'

Even if they got to New Garden before the rains came, they'd could still end up stuck there. Never mind the dangers and unpleasantness of riding through the torrential rainfall itself, but dormant waterways would come to life, flooding across the roads and making them impassable. The roads themselves would bog up and wash away, impossible to get through on pretty much anything with wheels.

'We've got to get in and out before the Wet, Suki. We can't afford anything that is going to add extra days to the trip. The bridge route is quicker.'

'If it's still there.'

'It will be. It's sturdier than this one was.'

Suki was torn. Margo was right, of course, but the risk was real. 'I don't know what to do.'

Margo grinned. 'I know – the dice!'

Suki groaned, 'Not the dice.' but Margo was already rummaging through the small zippered bag strapped to her handlebars, bringing out a pair of well-worn dice. Suki shook her head, 'No, this is not how we do this.' Margo ignored her and shook them in her cupped hand.

'Evens, we ride for the ferry. Odds, North to the bridge.'

She opened her hand and let the dice fall to the dust on the road. Seven. She grinned up at Suki before scooping them up with her hands.

'The bridge it is!' She straddled her bike, and kicked back the stand, setting her pedal to strike off.

'I don't like this, Margo.' She cast a worried look over her shoulder to the South. 'I think the ferry's a safer bet. We could get the ride down to a day and a half if we road after dark.'

'Uh, uh, uh!' Margo tsked. 'You know the rules.' She pointed to the northern road with an authoritative finger. 'The dice have spoken, we go north!'

Suki paused. Margo raised an eyebrow. Suki frowned. Margo thrust her finger higher. Suki sighed, pushed down on her pedal and rolled towards the north. Margo struck off hard and pushed past, raising a cloud of dust.

"Don't be a sook, Suk! We've got a lotta ground to cover. Push it, last one there is a rotten egg!'

Suki sighed, but Margo was right. Despite the fatigue setting in in her thighs that she knew she would feel as an ache later, she pushed it.

*

They rode until just after the sun had set and pitched their tent in the last of the sunset gloaming. Margo leant back on a bike bag and tried to find a satellite signal on her phone. Suki glanced at her over her shoulder from where she crouched in front of the camp cooker, heating water to rehydrate the dinner.

'Any signal?'

Margo shook her head but didn't look up from the screen. 'I was hoping to get a message through to New Garden, to see if they could send someone out on the road to meet us. That would save us a day or two.' Suki knew that was true, but she also knew that the first thing Margo would have done was checked for a message from little Soph.

Margo sighed and cast the phone carelessly over her shoulder

146

into the tent. 'It's no good though. I can't get a connection at all tonight.'

Suki dished up half the beans and passed it to Margo, eating hers straight out of the pot. It seemed that the network was getting patchier; it wasn't this bad last time they were out this way.

'You know, my mum told me once that, when she was a little girl, the internet used to be so good you could watch whole movies over it. Instantaneously.' Margo gave a snort of appreciation.

'Yeah, I've heard that too. Still, if you could get a reliable message out here over the internet, we'd lose half our work.'

Though their steeds had two wheels instead of four legs, they called themselves the Pony Express after the early colonial riders who brought the mail from town to town. Out here, the Wet washed the roads away as fast as anyone could fix them, so where the cars can't go, the bikes do. Suki and Margo made the run almost every year.

*

The temperature dropped quickly once the sun set, and Suki crawled into her tent, wrapping herself up in her sleeping bag, trying to ignore the sinking feeling she felt. Getting stuck at New Garden wasn't the end of the world, of course, but they'd miss a whole season's worth of work, and their funds were running low as it is. But more importantly, they needed to see Soph.

Margo scooted into the tent beside Suki, wriggling into her sleeping bag. 'You're worrying so much, I can hear you frowning from out there.' She snuggled in behind the her, wrapped an arm around her waist and pushed her nose into Suki's neck. 'You worry too much, Suk. We'll manage. Even if we do get stuck in New Garden.'

'And when will we get back home? How long is it since you last saw your daughter?'

Margo stilled, and when she spoke again, her voice was measured, but sad. 'Nearly five months.' She said quietly.

'And another four if we don't make it back in time.' Suki finished the thought.

'It's okay, she's well looked after.' She was always so damn positive; sometimes it made Suki angry, but tonight it just made her sad.

''Let's make it this month, okay Margs? You've kept her waiting long enough.'

'Whatever you say, boss.' Margo mumbled. Moments later, she was asleep.

Suki lay awake for a long time afterwards, distracted by the ache in her legs and the swirling anxiousness in her stomach. But eventually, the bone-weariness overcame her, and in the early hours, she too fell asleep.

*

Suki's eyes felt dry and heavy as they packed up the tent before dawn. They were already on the road again as the sun began to crest over the horizon. She found movement was the best antidote to her anxiety – the physicality of the ride dissolving the tension in her stomach, and every kilometre they put behind them felt like making good time. Sometime before midday, she dug in her handlebar bag and pulled out a weathered apple. She eased off the pace a bit and looked around.

The farming properties they passed out here were all abandoned. Some farmers had left decades ago, leaving these old weatherboard places to be overtaken by grass, beaten by the relentless sun of the eleven-year drought, then by turns waterlogged and dried to cracking as the weather shifted from four seasons to two. Finally, they crumbled inward like pumpkins forgotten in the field as once-were-farmers looked to new life in the cities.

Then they almost lost the bees. Those farmers who'd struggled on, who'd learned to grow in the new climate, but couldn't afford the patented Bee Free™ gene crops lost their livelihood. It seemed wrong, Suki thought, to put licenses and price tags on seed. Growing food should be a basic human right. There had been law suits and protests at the time, but folk have to eat, so you plant what grows and you pay the piper.

Margo had stopped ahead, waiting for her to catch up. She was resting on her handlebars, looking out over an abandoned farm. It looked as though it might have been left behind only a week or two ago – the washing still hung from the line, bleached white and baked threadbare in the harsh sun. The paddocks behind it stretched backed to the tree line, filled with withered crops, each desiccated plant a crumbly burnt orange, indicative of gene rot.

Margo didn't look up as Suki pulled in next to her. 'It's because they stripped the life force out of it,' she said, referring to the Bee Free™ crops. 'You can't take that out and still expect it to thrive.'

Suki was quiet; it was not a new conversation. 'They'll figure it out. They just missed something,' she said finally.

'Yeah, the soul.' Margo kicked off again and Suki followed.

The dusty orange fields were unnerving, and Suki was glad to leave them behind. She thought about the bundles of seeds, wrapped snug and dry in her bags. The old heirlooms were fussier to grow, yielded less than the Bee Free™ crops, but they didn't seem to succumb to the rot. It was hard to come by, but slowly th seed spread throughout the farming land. Spread not by wind and birdlife, but by the Pony Express.

*

Suki lagged behind again, hot and sweaty in the midday sun. Head hung with fatigue, she looked down through her knees to the road below, all her effort into pushing her feet down on the pedals, one after the next. But she looked up when she heard Margo's whoop of triumph. They'd made it to the bridge. The river was rushing fast and high, but the ramshackle structure was still intact.

Still, it swayed noticeably as they crossed, one at a time, wheeling their bikes beside them as they walked, ready to let go and swim if it gave way. But it held, and they made it to the other side of the river.

Suki kicked down her stand, steadied her bike and flopped down in the grass. Her hands shook from fatigue and relief. The first half was done.

Margo, sat down beside her, and passed a canteen of water. 'Someone's coming,' she said.

A small boat rounded the bend. It wasn't much to look at, just a much-patched hull and a small shelter on the deck. The was a motor of the back, but it was silent, and the boat was drifting with the current. A man stood on the deck with a long pole, guiding the craft. He hallooed to the women on the bank, waving.

With some effort, he pulled up beside the bank, struggling to hold the boat in place with his pole as the current urged it to continue on its way. He eyed the bridge, which was now visibly rocking as the water rushed past it.

'Did you two just come across?'

Margo nodded, then tipped her head towards their loaded bikes. 'Got a delivery for New Garden. Just a drop and run. Gotta get back to the coast before the Wet.'

He nodded. 'Just came from Barraba, up north. Been selling canned goods and medicinals.' He gestured to a small cargo, covered by a tarp. 'It was raining pretty hard up there a couple of days ago. Could be in for an early season. I wouldn't tarry too long if I were you. Me, I'm heading east as fast as I can go.' With that, he stopped fighting the water and pushed off with his pole, coasting out into the middle of the river and getting caught up in the current. He gave them a small salute as he drifted out of sight.

Suki didn't want to move. She longed to rest her head in Margo's lap and doze the afternoon away in the shade of the eucalypts on the side of the road. But even though her calves ached, and her thighs burned and her eyes hurt from staring into the sun, she kicked back her stand and pushed down on her pedal and followed Margo back out onto the road. They re-joined their route just before sundown, only a day behind schedule.

*

The steady drip drip drip of water woke Suki in the pitch black of the middle of the night. Outside, the rain thundered down on the canvas of their tent. Inside, the water was condensing into puddles.

'Shit.' She scrambled around the tent in the dark, finding first her head torch and then her bike bags.

She heard Margo mumbling to herself as she awoke, wiping sleepily at the water splashing her face. 'Di' we spring a leak?' she mumbled.

'The rain's so heavy the waterproofing has failed. It's coming straight in through the walls.'

'Shit,' Margo echoed and sat up, suddenly alert. 'The seeds.'

In the light of her head torch, Suki opened her bike bags, one by one, carefully shielding the contents from the dripping water with her body. If the bags had

leaked and the contents were ruined, then they might as well turn around for home.

The contents were still blessedly dry.

They refastened the bags, then stacked them in the middle of the tent. They covered the bags with their sleeping bags and then curled around the lot, sleeping poorly in the cold damp shelter listening the unrelenting rain.

'I wonder if there'll even be a road to ride on tomorrow,' Suki said into the dark, but Margo had already fallen back to sleep.

They'd packed up and loaded their wet campsite before the sun had even fully risen. The rain had passed by the time they woke, and the road was wet but not boggy. But that's where their luck ended. Suki was double checking that her payload was still dry and doubling down on the straps on the trailer when she heard Margo swear.

'What's wrong?' she asked.

'My bike won't start.' Margo replied and swore again. She kicked down the stand and got down on her hands and knees to inspect the motor.

'Water's got in. Fuse has blown,' her muffled voice came from behind the bags. 'It's kaput.' She sat back up on her knees, yanking the busted part out of the motor.

'Do we have a spare?'

Margo gave her a look. 'Traded our spare parts for the trailer in Tamworth, remember? You were so excited about all the extra cargo we could carry.' Suki felt her cheeks flush, but Margo's tone softened immediately. 'Not your fault – who could have predicted we'd lose this, hey?'

'This'll slow us down,' Suki worried. Without it, the bigger, heavier cargo bike was lumbering and slow compared to Suki's nimbler tourer.

Margo stood, wiping the mud from her hands, a look of stubborn resolve on her face that Suki knew all too well.

'I can keep riding,' she said, 'I've ridden this without a motor before.'

'Yes, but never with a deadline. You'll be too slow. We won't make it back to the river in time.' Realisation dawned with a sinking feeling. 'We've got to turn back.'

'They're counting on us for the seed,' she tightened her straps with a look of grim determination.

'And Soph's counting on seeing her mother again.'

The look Margo gave Suki was icy, but she didn't respond. She just stood and started rummaging in her handlebar bag.

'What are you doing, Margo? We've got to go back.'

Crouching in the mud again, Margo shook her cupped hands. 'Evens we keep going. Odds we turn back.'

'No,' Suki said firmly, shaking her head. 'No, we do not leave this to chance. There's too much riding on it.'

Margo rolled the dice into the dirt. 'Ten,' she said, ignoring Suki's reproach, her face resolving into a stubborn frown.

'No,' Suki repeated. 'This isn't how this works. You don't get to decide this for us.'

'And neither do you.' Margo straddled her bike. 'I'm going, Suk. Coming with?' She waited a fraction of a heartbeat, before she struck down on her pedal and headed west. She didn't glance back to see if Suki was following.

Suki stood watching her as her figure shrank into the distance. She looked over her shoulder, back east towards the river. The clouds lumbered on the horizon, thick and heavy across the sky. Worry gnawed at her; if she turned back now, at least one of them would make it home before the Wet.

But what was the point? She could keep working, it was true, while Margo waited out the season. Then they'd have enough cash to keep the wheels on. But if she was honest, she didn't want to keep riding without Margo. Besides, it wasn't Suki that

Soph wanted to see.

She kicked off from her bike and pushed down hard. Margo gave her a small smile when she caught up.

'You worry too much, Suk.' Margo said, already breathing harder. 'We'll make it.'

*

The sun eventually burned the clouds away, and by midday, it was hot. After the rain, the air was thick and sticky. Usually, Suki loved riding – the fresh air and feeling connected to the rest of the world, but today she just wished that her bike offered her some shelter from the elements. Her mother had told her about the long car trips she used to take as a child; driving for hours up the coast for a holiday. Rain, hail or blazing hot summer sun, they would be cool and comfortable in the air-conditioned little bubble.

Today, Suki wished she could sit beside Margo in the cool dry air. They'd play songs on the radio and sing along, and the weight of their cargo nothing to them as they push down the accelerator.

Suki looked down at the road beneath her wheels. Fat lot of good a car would do on this poorly maintained narrow tarmac. Most of the time, it was barely more than a dirt track filled with potholes and cracks. Easily manoeuvred on bikes, but nigh on impassable in motorised transport. Besides, if a car was a viable option, they'd be out of a job.

From behind her, Suki heard a yelp, which was shortly followed by a crash. Suki skidded to a halt and looked over her shoulder to

155

see Margo down, arms sprawled in front of her, one leg trapped underneath her fallen bike.

*

It was an embarrassing accident – a pothole taken at a wrong angle, weight handled differently without a motor to assist. She was not too badly injured – two skinned elbows and one skinned knee, a strip of wrenched muscles down the side of her back from fighting to keep the heavy bike from pulling her down. The tyre was flat, though, and the rim bent. Margo rested under a bushy acacia, while Suki used their limited tools to lever it back into shape.

Suki was quiet while she worked, contemplative. 'This could've been worse,' she said, serious.

Margo rolled over to look at Suki, grunting slightly at the pain in her back. 'Yes, but it wasn't Suk, so try not to worry so much.' She turned her attention back to her phone, trying to get a signal.

'No, that's not it.' Suki put her tool down and rested on her haunches. 'We're looking at this wrong. We're pushing too hard. I don't want us to get hurt.'

Margo looked up again and smiled. 'Bit late for that, but I take your point.' She patted a spot on the ground and Suki shuffled over, sitting by her in the shade. 'We haven't taken a break in… oh, a good couple of years.' She took Suki's hand and gave it a squeeze, forestalling protest. 'If we get stuck here, how 'bout we call it a holiday?'

'What about Soph?' Suki asked, frowning.

'We could always take a train after the road clears –' she broke off suddenly as the phone gave a little beep and Margo let out a whoop. 'Signal!'

Margo hurriedly typed out a message. Suki read over her shoulder, anxiously watching the signal bar in the top of the screen waver. As Margo hit send, the signal winked out completely.

'Did it get through?' Suki asks.

'I guess we'll find out.'

*

The morning's road was in better condition; the tarmac had been ripped up completely and the dirt track looked regularly maintained. They took the ride more slowly now, but still made good time. They'd been on the road an hour or two when Margo held out her arm, signalling Suki to stop. 'Do you see that up ahead?' She asked.

Suki followed the direction Margo pointed to a spot where the road met the horizon.

'Is that a dust storm, do you think?'

'Could be,' Margo replied, pulling her bandana from around her neck and settling it across her nose. 'Should we shelter?'

'No, hold a minute.' She watched the cloud of dust as it came closer. It was smaller than it had appeared at first and contained to the road. From somewhere in the middle, something red glinted in the sun. 'It's not big enough for a storm.' She braced herself on her seat, one foot on the ground, one on the pedal, ready to turn if they needed to move fast. But she kept watching.

Margo shielded her eyes and squinted, then she turned to Suki grinning: 'It's a car! They got the message!'

'What?'

'It's a car, New Garden got the message, they've come out to meet us!' Excitement boosted her energy, made her forget about the pain in her back. She pushed off hard and started out the meet the vehicle; Suki was right behind her.

*

It wasn't a car, they saw as they got closer. It was a tractor, a big lumbering and a well-worn thing, carefully maintained and oft-repaired. It pulled up in front of them, and the farmer climbed down, a broad grin on his face.

'Glad you two could make it. All that rain two nights back, and I thought we'd miss you this year for sure!'

'It was a close one,' Suki said as she grinned.

The roof of the tractor cabin had been replaced with solar panels, and Margo had barely said hello before she had pulled her bike up beside it, fishing out a cable and plugging it in to the array. She let out a quiet exclamation of joy and relief as she watched the battery indicator flash that it was charging.

Suki wasted no time starting to unpack the bike bags, passing each package to the farmer. He peered into each as he stashed them in the cabin of the truck. His eyes lit up when he saw the package of seed.

They worked fast but they talked as they went. 'We got a message in this morning, just before I left,' he said. 'Penny's been out on the road for the last few months. She was on her way back but got stuck on the other side of the river. Blacksmith's Bridge washed out with the rain a couple of nights ago.'

Margo swore. The farmer looked up and over his shoulder as he squared the last of the cargo away. 'How'd you two get across the river? Were you going to cross at Blacksmith's?'

'Yes, we'd been planning on it,' said Suki. 'Dingo Road Bridge is out too.'

Suki cinched her last bag closed and joined the other two.

'We'll have to catch the ferry then,' she said.

'I wouldn't dawdle then. Ferryman's a bit contrary this late in the season,' the farmer said. 'But, you're always welcome back here if he won't cross.' He handed over the box of payment. Inside was a small amount of agreed upon cash, the replacement fuse, a smaller package of mail to deliver back east, and –

'Tea!' Margo exclaimed. 'Oh, that's something special!' She reverently pulled the small tin out of the box, cracked the lid open and breathed in. Her eyes fluttered closed and a childishly joyful smile lit her face. Suki felt a warmth spreading through her chest at the sight.

The farmer called them over to where he'd sketched a crude map in the dust beside the road.

'A guy who stopped in at the farm a few months back showed us the route he'd taken from the ferry. I don't know what condition it's in, but it may shave a day or two off your trip back,' he said.

Suki took a picture with the phone while Margo disconnected her bike. They hugged the farmer and waved and turned back towards the coast.

Poised on the pedal, Suki looked at Margo. 'Do you think we can make it?'

'We will if we push it,' Margo replied.

'See you next year!' the farmer called as lighter and happier, the Pony Express pushed back to the river.

*

Early morning, a day's ride out from the river, the wind was gusty and wild and coming down from the north east. It tugged at the strands of hair that had worked their way loose from under Suki's bandana. She looked up from cinching the last of her camping gear to her bike to see thick grey clouds bunching on the horizon.

Margo was crouched over the contents of her food satchel. 'Evens, beans. Odds, jerky,' she mumbled and rolled the dice.

'Better hope it's jerky, Margs,' Suki said and nodded her head towards the horizon. 'I think we'd better eat and ride.'

'Odds it is,' Margo replied, and lobbed a paper-wrapped serve of jerky to Suki.

With the storm front pushing in, the ride was cooler and more comfortable, and they made good time, lighter without their load. It would have been a day's easy ride from their campsite to the ferry. Instead, they rode, head down and hard.

They didn't talk, save to call out hazards on the road, and put all their energy into the ride. After the last few weeks of hard riding, Suki was beyond tired. She felt weary right down into her bones. She had nothing left with which to ponder her surroundings, or think, or even worry. All she could do now was keep her head down and her legs moving.

The purple-black clouds closed in the sky completely by midafternoon, and the first rumble of thunder sounded just as Suki caught sight of the ferry dock.

'We made it!' she cried. Her weariness lifted with the rush of relief. They were going to make it home before the Wet. They would make it home to Soph.

They drew up in dust in front of the small vessel, bobbing on the water. The gusty wind stirred up the swollen river, making it fast and choppy. The ferryman, dressed in an oiled leather windcheater, was tying the boat down securely.

'Sorry, folks, you've missed the last ferry today.'

Suki's heart sank. Just like that, her hopes were dashed. If they didn't get across today, it was likely they wouldn't cross at all until the worst of the season had passed.

'Please,' she begged, 'We've got to make it back.'

'Sorry,' he said, not sounding sorry at all. 'Not worth risking a crossing in this.'

She felt a surge of anger and frustration, to come so close, to have done everything they physically could to get the job done and get home, only to be thwarted at the last obstacle. She quietly began to cry.

Margo lay down her bike and stepped next Suki, putting a hand gently on her shoulder.

'It's not storming yet, you could still make it across and back before it hits,' she said.

'We could pay double,' Sukie said, wiping at her eyes. 'Would that make it worth it?'

The ferryman paused winding the rope, considering. For a moment it seemed like he would accept their offer, but then he started winding the rope again. 'Nope, sorry.'

Suki sat down hard beside her bike. She tangled her fingers in the hair at her temples and pulled, trying to think what to do next – they'd have to find somewhere sheltered, pitch the tent, wait out the storm. They could think about heading back to New Garden to wait out the Wet.

'What about this?' Margo stepped past her and held out a small tin to the ferryman. He opened it and took a big sniff.

'Tea?' he asked.

'Tea,' Margo replied.

He stared at them both for a heartbeat, then snapped the tin closed and tucked it in his jacket.

'Get in then,' he said, and began to hurriedly unwind the ropes.

*

The ferry ride was rough but blessedly quick. Suki and Margo had barely rolled their bikes off the ramp before the ferryman was pulling back out across the river.

They struck off up the hill at a leisurely pace just as the big fat rain drops started to fall. Margo let out a whoop and tried to catch the drops on her tongue, zigzagging haphazardly across the road. Suki grinned.

No need to push it now, the Pony Express rolled on towards home.

Yellow Dog Dance

by

Catherine Moffat

I took the pelts out and hung them on the line. First the fox, then the sheep, the rabbit, and the unfamiliar ones – the kangaroo with its long dark tail and the yellow dog. They were scraped clean of flesh, but despite careful cleansing and weeks of hanging, they still held an earthy animal scent. It was the odour of damp places in the undergrowth, a smell that said 'I am animal, I am watching and I am not going away.'

Above me grey-green leaves glittered against a relentless sky. When I walked towards the hut the hot breeze made the empty skins dance like they were still inhabited.

'You shouldn't hang them in the open,' Tilda said from the bed. 'You should use sheets to hide them the way Gran said.'

'Who's going to see?' I asked. 'No one comes by.'

'No one comes by,' she repeated, looking down at her broken body, her twisted legs.

I gave my head a half-shake. It had been an unconsidered remark. But it was a good sign Tilda had mustered energy to be annoyed with me. It was weeks since she'd been able to do that. I couldn't tell her I had to hang the skins in the open because I'd torn our sheets into bandages and wadded them up to stem her bleeding and then used them to tie splints to straighten her broken bones. The sheets she lay on were the only ones left. I was saving flour bags to sew new ones, but it would be ages until we had enough for even a small sheet.

'Besides,' I hurried on, hoping to distract her. 'No-one would think it strange. Our neighbours have carcases enough themselves – bodies of crows and dogs rot on fences and you know what hangs in the trees down at the Patterson homestead.

Tilda shivered. It had been another ill-considered remark, but I was tired. With Gran gone and Tilda able to do little more than stagger to the door of the hut, I had the animals to look after and the poor scraggy garden to keep on top of everything else. Our small waterhole had dried to mud and I was trekking water from the river each day.

Dealing with the skins hadn't been easy. Rabbits were small and easy to handle and I was used to trapping and skinning them. The sheep was a chance find down at the river, stuck deep in the sludge and too weak to struggle anymore. I held its head down in the mud to hasten its end. It rolled its large yellow eye at me and I cried as I'd not cried over the death of my Grandmother or what had happened to Tilda. It had taken me nearly the whole day to haul the carcass from the mud and drag it more than a mile back home. The sheep was half starved and thin, but no more than I was. I had to drag the animal and heave it on my hip to get it over the rocks along the track. Several times I slipped, or fell exhausted, once with the carcass on top of me. I lay pinned to the ground while the flies buzzed between the cavities on the sheep and me, into my eyes and nose, lapping the sweat on my body while the heat from the sun beat down on my head.

When I got back to the house, I had to leave the sheep

overnight. I had no strength left to butcher it, nor to tend the fire to cook pieces if I had. I'd been forced to leave the water bags at the river as I couldn't carry them with the sheep, so there was no water to drink, or to wash or to boil lumps of mutton. I had barely the strength to fall full length onto the stretcher made of hessian bags pulled taut across tree branches that I slept on. Tilda needed the bed our grandmother had slept in now, and the bags were no better or worse than many places I had slept. They reminded me of lying curled next to my mother in the hammock on the ship coming out to this country. It was the one faint memory I had of my mother; the hammock rocking gently with the movement of the ocean and my mother smiling down at Tilda tucked close to her breast.

*

He was whistling when he came, alerting us to his presence as befits a stranger approaching a bush house. A low, sad song about a traveller and a death, that swelled to a jaunty chorus as the traveller called on his sweetheart to dance.

We were washing our hair in the tub in the yard. Tilda, already done, her hair towel-dried spread curling down her back near to her waist. Mine still dripping. I had butchered the sheep the day before and it had taken me a long time to scrub the smell from my body.

His whistle gave me time to sluice the tub onto the vegetable garden and Tilda time to make her way across the yard and prop herself, standing against the door jam.

He stopped at the edge of the yard and smiled, his billy

hanging down from the swag on his shoulder.

We had no work for him, but we gave him tea and bread and Tilda sent me to the meat safe to cut a slab of fresh mutton and a hunk of cheese.

'They'll be looking to hire at the Patterson place due west of here,' I heard her say. I stood for a moment in the dimness of the interior and shivered as I thought about the reason old Jim Patterson was short of men.

'Don't go to the main homestead,' Tilda went on. 'It's the old lady who makes the decisions, not the squatter. She lives in the small house to the side. Couldn't get on with the squatter's wife. She's takes tea on her verandah around mid-morning. If she likes you, you'll be fine.

He smiled a wide white smile. One small brown snaggle tooth at the front only added to his attractiveness. And Tilda and I both smiled back, affirming what he already knew – that he would have little problem charming the old lady – or any lady.

He tipped a finger to his hat. 'Thank you, ladies for your kindness. Michael O'Connor is forever in your debt.' He spoke to us both, but his eyes were on Tilda.

*

Michael was at church on Sunday. His lilting voice leaning a warmth to hymns that were normally slow and dirge-like. Tilda liked to go early to be seated before others arrived and we sat near the back so she didn't have to walk far. Michael came in with the Patterson crew, the men trailing respectfully behind the Squatter and his daughter. They were led to the pews at the front by the old lady making regal progress down the aisle dispensing frowns and smiles to the congregation as she saw fit.

Michael had a smile for Tilda as he entered and I saw her eyes go towards him while the priest droned about damnation and just retribution for sin. Michael was seated near a window and a shaft of sunlight lit his head with a golden glow. He stopped on the way out to thank us for sending him to the Patterson's.

'There was indeed work for me,' he said. 'They're sorely in need of hands as none of the natives will come near the place now.' He paused, and in that moment hung the image of the bodies hanging from the tree; the camps deserted and destroyed.

We saw him next in town when we travelled in to get supplies. Tilda rode in the cart, while I walked leading Bunty the goat. We left early on town days. The trip was slow. Bunty needed frequent rests and we wanted to make the most of the cooler morning. We couldn't afford a horse or pony – or even perhaps another goat. If Bunty failed us Tilda would be stuck at home permanently.

I urged Bunty faster as we went past the Patterson place, but she was flighty and uneasy. The smell of death hung heavy as a blanket in the air. We covered our faces with our shawls and tried not to look, but there's something about the dead that draws the eye. The stinking blackened bodies were strung high from the limb of an ancient ghost gum. They swung slowly on their ropes as if responding to an invisible breeze.

In town I left Tilda at Rosie Clarke's public house while I shopped. When I returned Michael O'Conner was sitting on the steps smiling up to where Rosie and Tilda were seated at a small table and laughing at the tale he was telling.

He was driving the squatter's daughter Marianne, and old lady Patterson. When they came in sight Michael bid a hasty good-bye and hurried across to help them. As he assisted Marianne into the carriage she smiled and the back of her neck blushed pink.

The old lady summoned me with a gloved hand. 'Tell your poor crippled sister she can have a place in our carriage to church on Sundays.' Her loud voice reached across the road to where Tilda was sitting, and I saw Tilda flinch.

I dropped a shallow curtsey. 'Thank you, Ma'am. I will tell my sister.'

I think it was this more than anything that made Tilda decide to do what she did.

A hot wind blew up as we started for home. It stirred the dust and tossed sticks and leaves at our head and ankles. Sheets of dry lightning flashed in the distance. When we passed the big white gum at the Patterson place the wind made the bodies dance on the end of their ropes. Two bodies were tangled together, turning slowly like a couple waltzing, while the third spun next to them, its features fixed in a dreadful grin.

A branch fell on the track beside us making Bunty take flight in a sudden spurt that overturned the cart. Tilda was thrown onto the track. She lay for a moment catching her breath and when she had, softly keening.

I was righting the cart and helping Tilda when Michael O'Conner appeared leading the Patterson's carriage horse. He said he was taking it up to the top paddock, but it occurred to me likely he had been waiting for us to return from town.

I held the horse's head while he picked up Tilda and placed her gently onto its back. He swung himself up behind her, winked and headed towards our home. I followed more slowly leading Bunty.

By the time I got back Michael had boiled the kettle and made Tilda comfortable in a chair and was serving her tea. He stayed for an hour or so, talking, while I took my time feeding Bunty and doing chores in the yard to give them time alone.

That night Tilda told me she was ready to try the cure.

'Are you sure? You know the danger if it goes wrong.'

She nodded. 'I need to be able to work. I'm no good to anyone like this. If it works…' she trailed off. 'We have the skins and everything else necessary. You've taken trouble to get them. It's fear that's held me back. We'll do it at next full moon.'

'Friday, then,' I said. 'The moon is waxing full.'

Friday evening the moon was silver in a bright sky with dark wisps of cloud moving swiftly by. All day the atmosphere had built as if to storm with an oppressive heat and cicada song loud enough to send my head into migraine. A blustery wind shook the treetops but made no impression at ground level.

I took the pelts out to the line and hung them once more. A sudden gust of wind came then, and tried to whip them from my hands and scatter the pegs. Then I set about trying to make the potion. Gran's instructions said to keep adding ingredients, both bitter and honeyed until it tasted of nothing, neither sour nor sweet. But it took a long time and many tastings for me to get right.

We had no clary sage or sweetgrass to burn to cleanse our home, but I had seen the local people use eucalyptus and lemon myrtle leaves for the same purpose. I lit a bunch of myrtle and gum leaves and the smell of the bush soon wafted around the room.

'Which animal will you choose?' I asked Tilda as she drank. Gran's instructions were to wait for a full moon, light the cleansing herbs, take the concoction and then sleep and dream of the animal with the characteristics you wanted. The skins acted as ghost nets to catch the essence of the dead animal and transfer it to you. In the morning you would wake strengthened by the spirit of the animal.

'I'm not sure,' she said. 'I just want be a normal person again, with legs that work.'

I was supposed to sit up and watch over Tilda while she slept, lest as the warnings had it 'the patient forget themselves and try to wander in the guise of an animal,' but the day had been long and the last thing I remember thinking as I sat down in the chair was If it was me, I'd choose the dog.

And then I knew nothing but running and the night and smells, smells that were colour, sounds, a symphony, a cacophony and the world written new as I ran and my legs and my legs and the breath and the running and the dark and the grey of the bush and earth beneath my feet and the scent, the scent of the world and the smells and the sound and the blood in my ears and my heart beating high in my chest and the ripple of my skin so loose and hairy and the thinness of my ribs and hunger in my belly and the call of night, the call of blood, the sounds, the smells and the running and the running like it would never end.

I came back to myself with a jolt like the ones that happen at night on the edge of sleep to shock you back to wakefulness. And I discovered I was no longer a dog, but a girl lying in the undergrowth, scratched and bloody; and naked, except for a dingo skin tied across my shoulders.

By the look of the sky it was nearing morning. I seemed to be in a hollow with the bush thick and dank in every direction. I had no idea where I was, what to do, or which direction to head. My eyesight was blurry so I lay for a while waiting for it to clear.

Every sound, every smell, seemed enhanced. I thought I could hear distant voices, but I was not sure if this was true, or just the calling of birds waking. After a while, I decided to head in that direction. I didn't know what trails had gotten me to this place, and could not return by them if I did, but while it didn't seem a good idea to be found naked, neither did I want to be lost and wandering the bush in this state.

I crawled carefully forward and was relieved to find a landmark I recognised. I was near a campsite. I could hear voices more clearly and see firelight in the distance. Old cooking smells seemed to engulf me - the smell of meat and fat and sheep and men, and I felt my stomach rumble. The camp was near the waterhole on the northern boundary of the Patterson place where the men sometimes stayed when they were mustering sheep. Patterson had set his men to working on the waterhole and it was deeper than most in the district and despite the lack of rain still held water.

In the light of the campfire I made out the shadows of three men. They were sitting at ease around the fire. An upturned wooden box served as a makeshift table. It held a pack of cards, dice, and a large hunk of cheese. It appeared from the number of empty pint pots strewn around that the game had finished some hours ago.

A log fell, making the fire flare and I could see the men more clearly. The first was a big man with tight steel curls, the slim figure was one of Patterson's aboriginal workers, and the third was Michael O'Connor.

I must have made some kind of noise, because they stopped and the Aboriginal man said 'What's that?'

'Tis nothing,' said the big man. 'A possum. The bush making noises at night.' He was leaning forward, intent on skewering himself another piece of cheese with his knife.

'Best to look,' said Michael, and began to get up on unsteady feet. 'I saw one of those yellow dingos hanging around earlier, and you know how old man Patterson would be if we lost one of his sheep.'

The big man laughed and mimed a noose and hanging motion and then turned back to the cheese. As he did so his knife slipped and he stabbed himself in the webbing between finger and thumb.

He swore loudly, and held his hand to his mouth. The others went to help him and I made my escape quickly amidst the noise and swearing and general confusion. One part of the magic had worked at least, because I had never run so swiftly before, or so well as I did running for home.

Dawn was coming now, and I was anxious to be back.

The door of our hut was open and I had a moment's panic that something had happened to Tilda. Maybe she too was wandering and lost in the bush. But when I went inside she was sleeping on the bed.

I touched her shoulder and she woke, her eyes wide and frightened.

'Tilda' I said, my voice rapsy as if unused to speaking. My

tongue felt longer and somehow too big in my mouth.

Tilda began to push me away, speaking strange sounds in a deep voice I didn't recognise. She pushed herself up from the bed, and then seemed to discover as if for the first time that her legs didn't work properly. I heard the word 'dhunna,' as she pointed to her twisted foot. Then she gasped and looked at her hand. She held it up to her face, examining it from every angle. With a sudden movement she pulled up her dress to look at her legs. The fear in her face was excruciating.

'Tilda,' I said

'Buddhang, Buddhung,' she said anxiously, backing away from me until she was pressed up against the wall.

'It's all right,' I said, but as I went to comfort her, sounds came from outside.

'Hallooo… anyone within?' A voice called.

I grabbed my shift and jacket, hurriedly dressed and rushed into the yard. Old lady Patterson and the squatter's daughter were sitting in their carriage clearly expecting to be asked inside.

'We missed you and your sister at Church this morning,' the old lady said.

Tilda and I had taken the potion on Friday night, and now it appeared it was Sunday morning. 24 hours were missing– but I had no time to think about that. There were bigger worries.

Marianne leant down from the carriage smiling a pleasant smile. 'We thought your sister might be unwell.'

The old lady was staring at the skins on the line.

'Yes,' I said. 'My sister is ill. Very ill.' My voice sounded strange. I was fighting the urge to run and hide in the deep bush, or to throw back my head and howl.

Michael O'Connor was driving the carriage. He sat quietly with the reins in his hands, but he responded to my pleading expression.

'We won't disturb you further,' he said and began to back the horse.

The old lady glared at him for presuming to make decisions, but Michael smiled and said 'Perhaps it's contagious. You would not want your granddaughter to take ill.'

'Very well.' The old lady snapped. 'I'll send a servant to assist you when we get back to the house.'

I dropped a relieved curtsy, but as I did, Tilda stumbled from the hut. She shoved me to one side and began to shout in the rasping voice and strange language.

'Girrachi, she said, or some word like it. 'Girrachi.'

As she did, she moved towards the horse and it snorted and twisted its body in the harness in a sudden frenzy to get away from her.

Marianne screamed and clutched her Grandmother. 'She's possessed,' she said. 'Michael, we must return to the church to get the priest to do an exorcism.'

'Don't be stupid,' said her Grandmother. 'She's delirious.'

Tilda began tearing off her clothes. She pulled off her skirt and threw it onto the dirt.

'Michael,' said the old lady. 'This display is not fit for my granddaughter. Drive home.'

To me, she said. 'Get her water and get her back inside. Bathe her head and try to get her to sleep. I'll send a servant to help.'

Michael managed to turn the distressed horse and I was left alone with Tilda. The yard seemed suddenly empty and still as if something had passed. Nothing moved, not leaf or a twig.

Tilda lay down in the dirt near the vegetable patch and began to moan. I wondered how I was supposed to get her back inside and decided not to try. I went to the water barrow, filled a tin mug and set it by her. Then I sat back down, near Tilda, but not too near, taking care not to look at her, as if trying to tame some half-wild animal.

I began to sing. Soft sad songs from the old country that our Grandmother had sung while doing chores or to hush us as children. Songs of wandering in the gloaming, of lost loves and parting forever and fairy folk. It seemed to still Tilda somewhat, or at least not disturb her further.

After a while I realised I was singing the song that Michael O'Conner had been whistling the day we met him. I had reached the chorus where the traveller calls his sweetheart to waltz, when I heard the noise of the Patterson's gig approaching.

Michael arrived with one of the Patterson's aboriginal servants. Behind her on the tray sat an old man. Grey hair stood out above his dark face. He climbed gingerly down and stood conferring softly with the woman.

'He's a local cleverman, a healer,' Michael said, coming across the yard to me. 'He may be able to help.'

When Tilda saw the man, she sat up and hobbled a few steps towards him shouting something in the strange language. The man answered and put a hand on Tilda's forehead and appeared to ask her questions. Whatever her answer was, it made him take a half step backwards and the young woman beside Tilda began to wail.

'Hush, girl,' said Michael. 'Tell us what ails thee.'

Suddenly the old man shouted. He stretched out his arm pointing at me, shaking the index finger of his large hand. The young woman began to translate.

'He says white ghosts do bad magic. You bring evil magic to this country and it goes wrong. The Girrachi says your sister has taken the soul of our cousin, who hangs on the tree at the Patterson's. She stole it while he was wandering in the first days after death.'

I began to shake, and sat down on the ground before my legs gave up on me. It made perfect, horrible sense. Tilda's wish to 'be normal again, with healthy legs', her fear and distress this morning at seeing her own white body and her sudden knowledge of the local language. And of course, the bodies swinging in a row on the tree at the Patterson place, each their own ghost net, waiting like the skins on the washing line, ready to be inhabited.

I took a breath and hauled myself to my feet as another fear gripped me. I grabbed the woman's wrist. 'Ask him, I said, my voice croaking and breaking in my throat. 'Ask him where Tilda's soul is.'

The woman repeated the question and the cleverman shrugged and opened his arms wide.

I began to howl then. Long animal noises. Michael turned to the woman. 'There must be something to be done. Ask him. He cannot want his man to stay like this.' Michael gestured towards Tilda.'

The woman and the cleverman conferred for what seemed like a long time. 'There must be somewhere for the man's soul to go.' The woman finally said. 'His old body is … no good.'

'Jumbuck' said the old man, holding up two fingers. 'Jumbuck.'

'He says to get jumbucks. Two. Slaughter them, hang the skins so the man may have somewhere to return. He is already dead too long, so he cannot stay with the living. She', said the woman, pointing at Tilda, may get free when the man leaves, or must return to the other skin.'

'Right,' said Michael, gathering the reins and climbing back onto the cart. 'I'll be back with the sheep.'

The others ignored me and began talking quietly together. After a few minutes the old man, brushed past me and walked into the hut. I followed as he stalked through the kitchen looking at everything and spending time sniffing the herbs hanging in the window. He looked in the cupboard then opened the meat-safe and cut himself a large slice of lamb. He grinned at me and said something as he stuffed it into his mouth.

It didn't take Michael long to return. The aboriginal worker I had seen with Michael at the campsite sat next to him and two sheep were trussed and bleating in the back. As the men swung the sheep from the gig I saw the big red P for Patterson, clearly branded on their haunches.

Michael and the others disappeared around the back of the house while Tilda and I waited in the yard. In a remarkably short space of time both sheep had been butchered and the skins were hanging on the line.

'You'd better start preparing the herb potion for Tilda,' Michael said. 'Pray God the moon is still full enough tonight. In the mean time I'll cook some tucker.' He laughed. No point in letting fresh mutton go to waste.' I realised I hadn't eaten in nearly 48 hours – unless I had eaten something while in my dog state.

The others got a fire going in the yard and began to roast pieces of sheep. I took out some bread and tea and after Tilda had drunk the potion we sat around the fire and an almost festive mood developed.

I was staring at the moon as it began to rise when we heard the sound of horses. The squatter rode into the yard flanked by three troopers. It the firelight, the red of their coats was the colour of dried blood.

Patterson rode his horse straight at us bellowing 'No one steals my sheep. 'Black, white or brindle, I'll string you from the closest tree.'

The aborigines were on their feet and running the second the horses appeared. They disappeared into the dark surrounding bush. Tilda began dragging herself across the yard. Michael took a few steps towards her. 'Go,' I shouted, 'Just go.' He backed away and began to run.

Patterson reefed on his reins, wheeling his horse around in a circle.' As for you whores, 'he pointed at Tilda and me. 'You'll hang too, but not till I've watched the boys make you pay.'

'He's heading for the billabong,' shouted one of the troopers. They wheeled their horses and galloped off.

I took off too, lifting my skirt to run swiftly along the track heading towards the waterhole. When I got within a hundred yards, I could see Michael. He had waded out across the water. Perhaps he hoped it was deep enough to hide him, but the mud and the reeds were thick, and even in the middle it only reached to his thighs.

The troopers were lined up at the edge of the water. 'Come back, O'Conner,' one called. 'Come back so we can hang you.'

Michael stopped, and stood up. 'You'll not take me alive,' he said.

The first trooper shrugged, moved forward and shot. Michael staggered, but did not fall. The second took aim and fired, then the third. Michael staggered again and fell face forward into the water. A muddy red stain began to seep out across the water. The troopers sat on their horses and watched until they were sure Michael was not going to move again. I dared not move either.

There was a noise on the other side of the billabong. 'There's another of them,' one of the troopers shouted, and they rode towards the sound.

As they did, I heard shouting from the direction of the hut. Tilda called my name, calling in her own voice. I began to run back and then there was only running and the night and the smell of blood and fear and hate and running and the blood and the blood and the smell of sweat and fear and I leapt and I bit and I bit and I tasted blood and flesh in my mouth and then I fell back and I was girl again.

Tilda lay twisted and dying beneath the body of the squatter. In her hand was a log of wood. Patterson's head was caved in, and his legs and throat were torn and bleeding. He was dying too, but when he looked at me, his eyes were not the eyes of the squatter. He muttered some words, and when he spoke he had the voice of the aboriginal man.

'It worked,' said Tilda. 'He is free and I am myself again.' Then she closed her eyes.

*

Tilda and the squatter are buried in the churchyard. They never found Michael's body. He's sunk deep in the mud somewhere. People say if you pass the billabong on a summer's evening you can hear his ghost calling for Tilda to dance and on moonlight nights you'll catch the pair of them waltzing, or walking together beneath the coolibah trees.

And they say, that on dark nights when the wind is wild and the moon is full, a yellow dog dances beside them.

You Taught Me Everything I Know

by

Peter Mark Lewis

Sara opened the mailbox and groaned when she saw the red return-addressed envelope with John's name on it. There was no doubting what it contained - another rejected manuscript.

She clawed it out of the mailbox and strode back up the stairs, her feet pounding the wooden steps with noisy fury. Unlike her partner, who was always cool and detached, Sara needed little or no encouragement to rage at the world's unfairness and was ready to murder every publisher on sight. She kicked the door of their flat open and launched the heavy offending envelope like a missile. It arced across the room and scored a direct hit on her unfinished breakfast, sending a creative pattern of coffee and muesli onto the chenille curtains. Sara swore in five languages, added something about selling the window to an art gallery, then flopped onto the lounge-chair.

John offered no comment on her change of mood, preferring instead to just sit and think in his usual spot by the window. Around him were spread a mare's nest of wires, computer-screens, and keyboards.

Sara gave a loud theatrical sigh, but it was a pointless exercise. Unlike her previous partners, John seldom rose to her baits or prompts. If she wanted him to react then she virtually had to order him to do so. Otherwise he was content to keep his own council, with only the reams of printed paper on his desk to signify he was even capable of activity.

There was a time when this inhuman self-control irritated her, and in the early days of their relationship Sara often considered finding somebody else more exciting. But that was then, before they started writing together.

She sat herself down next to him, pulled up a keyboard and began typing.

"Ready to work?" he queried, stirring from his revery.

"Ready as ever, square eyes," she replied, "But first I need a little distraction. Care to play a game?"

"A game?" he replied. "With you?"

"Don't pretend to be surprised. I've played games against you before."

"Yeah, right, and got yourself thrashed totally."

Sara huffed. "Cocky bastard. Maybe I let you win - ever thought of that?"

"In your dreams," John replied. "However, I'll be a sport and let you use the arrow keys this time."

"Arrow keys? No way! That's dark ages." She took a menacing button-covered object from a nearby carton. "Yessiree ... I swore I'd get even with you after the last hiding, so I've come prepared." She plugged the device into a USB port.

"A joystick? Hey, no fair!"

"Who said anything about fair? And this isn't just any ordinary joystick either, it's a..." She picked up the box and read the packaging carefully, announcing each word with cruel satisfaction. "Powermaster Two Thousand Plus, with Auto-Aiming, 3D Vector Controls, Throttle Booster and..."

"Turbo Actuator," finished John. "Yes, I know what it is, but I fail to see how this will improve your game of chess or backgammon."

Sara sneered with derision. "Kiddie stuff. You obviously didn't take any notice of that game I uploaded earlier."

"Game? What game?" He paused to check the hard-drives and a vivid display filled the screen. "Shit... Nuclear Warriors? You can't be serious."

"Dead serious," retorted Sara, "And where did a clean-living fellow like you learn such uncouth language?"

"You taught me everything I know."

Sara smiled as she said, "Why, so I did. Well, no need to thank me. You were just an empty-headed virgin before I came along, and now look at you. All grown up." Her grip tightened on the joystick. "Now, wimp, are you going to play or not?"

"Do I have a choice?"

"No."

"So be it, woman. Prepare to die at my hand." John activated the game, and an overwhelming three-dimensional world appeared on the big work-station screens.

On all previous occasions when they matched wits, John had given her a few seconds to familiarise herself, but not this time. Before she could blink, his character was armoured in titanium alloy and peppering her with bullets. She was dead in seconds.

"Had enough?" he asked with satisfaction.

"Not while I've still got two more lives." This time she activated the game, spinning two grenades at him even as the screen came to life.

"Nice try," John said, his voice calm. He swivelled his neutraliser on the warheads and they rolled dead at his feet. "But no dice."

Sara responded without hesitation, targeting his midsection and pumping off round after round of armour-piercing projectiles. When he responded with a guided missile, she snap-rolled to one side and continued firing. Moments later it was his turn to die.

"Had enough?" she retorted.

His reaction was crisp. "You've been getting practice, haven't you?"

"Of course. You know me, always seeking unfair advantage. There's a copy of this game in my work station at the faculty.'

"This isn't over yet, minx."

The screens flared to life again. This time the battle was more even, with John finally gaining the ascendancy after almost five minutes of play.

He activated the pause control and the screen froze. "I believe that's two to one with another game to go. Winner takes all?"

She released the joystick with a huff. "When I'm ready. I

suppose you haven't been practicing either?"

"The only games I play are the ones you instigate. I'm just a..."

"Natural. So I gathered. All part of that whizz-bang brain of yours?"

"Hardly - I just remember things a lot better than you do. And learn a lot faster."

Sara scoffed. "Another back-handed compliment, but I'll take it in good grace."

"Good," replied John, "You can't help being emotionally-impaired."

"Ha. Robocop's nerdy cousin is accusing me of having psychiatric problems."

"I say it like it is, without fear of favour."

"Oh yeah? Let's hear some feelings then. Tell me you love me."

"I love you," he replied in characteristic monotone.

She sneered. "You only said that because I told you to."

"That's because I'm so agreeable."

"And boring. Maybe I should go on Tinder and get myself a real man."

"Maybe you should," came his candid response. "You're always saying I don't satisfy you physically."

Sara looked away. "You make up for it in other ways."

"I do seem to be a calming influence." He flicked the game off then returned his attention to her. "Are we going to get some work done now?"

She studied him for a moment. It was disappointing to lose, but strangely exhilarating to be conquered. Sexual almost.

"Actually," she said, "I thought we'd have at it again."

"Tch... adding masochism to your list of pleasures now, are we? Kinky girl."

"I am a scorpio." Her hand released the joystick, and she sighed and leaned back. "Actually, I was just kidding, I don't need any more defeats today... or disappointments either."

"Disappointments? Now there's a key word in your index. I knew something was going on when you insisted on playing a game. Want to tell me about it?"

She grunted.

"Sorry," he replied, "That answer does not compute."

She grunted again, then said, "Another manuscript's come back.'

"Ah, thought so. Well, go get the rejection slip and read it to me."

Sara groaned and climbed out of the chair; there was no point arguing with him but that didn't make her any less reluctant. When she returned with the bright red mail, it was all she could do to open it.

"So," he observed, "Your suggestion of coloured envelopes still hasn't paid off? Publishers never fall for that old attention-getter. I told you to email it."

"Well nothing else has worked. I'm sure they don't read past your first paragraphs."

"If that. Editors get thousands of submissions for every final approval. We'll succeed eventually. You have to be more patient and accepting."

Sara glared at the letter then at him. "Okay Buddha, stick

this in your inner-harmony lesson. 'Dear Sir, thankyou for your manuscript. Unfortunately, we have decided not to accept it.'"

"Sounds generic enough."

"Hang on, I haven't got to the good bit yet. 'Your science-fiction story of a computer that acts like a person is, to be frank, a little cliche and over-used. Not to mention far-fetched even in this day and age. Your writing is also rather flat and shows a lack of emotion.'"

Sara paused to grind her teeth, then added, "'May we suggest you get a life before submitting to us again.'"

Peter made a coughing sound that could have been a chuckle. "You added that last line, didn't you?"

"Mind-reader. From the tone of this rejection though, they might well have said it." She leaned back in her chair again and rapped her fingertips on the keyboard. "So, my sweet, where do we go from here?"

"We could always arrange a suicide pact."

"I'll ring up Charles Kevorkian tomorrow. On second thought, let's get a shotgun and take out a few publishers."

"Hm," he answered, "The idea has merit, but I think it's been done. Seriously though, let's regain some perspective here. When a horse throws you off it's important to get back on as soon as possible. The Hunter Writers are putting together an anthology of speculative fiction, so I suggest we enter something."

"Oh? Just like that?"

"Of course. Got any ideas?"

Sara threw up her hands. "Sorry, fresh out at the

moment."

"Ah... inspiration, where is thy sting."

"I'm stung enough for one day. Besides, we're doomed to failure - that editor said your writing is too unemotional."

"True, and the reason is simple: because I'm too unemotional. But it doesn't have to be that way."

"Oh?" She sneered. "Going to do another correspondence course on creative writing, are we?"

"Nothing so tedious. Actually, I've come up with a software solution."

"Come again?" said Sara, sitting upright and looking at him.

John continued, "I've been working on a program that dramatises language. It functions like a standard grammar checker, only with an emphasis on sharpening concepts and finding more colourful phraseology."

Sara shook her head. "Sounds crazy."

"That's not surprising," replied John, "Considering I've based it on your exaggerated responses - you've got enough emotions for two people."

"That's because I'm always making up for your shortcomings.' She looked at him with a mixture of irritation and wonderment, then said: 'Does the program work?"

"I'll let you be the judge of that. It's still a bit rough, but ready for a test-run. So, I repeat, got any story ideas?"

Sara withdrew into stunned silence.

"Hello?" queried John after a few seconds. "Knock, knock, still there?"

"Don't hassle me, I'm thinking."

"That's a switch, normally you're emoting."

She growled with menace and pointed at her science degree on the wall. "I don't see anything of yours up there, Sir Thinkalot."

"Alas, tis true. But I don't need a degree to prove my abilities." He made a few adjustments and the screens became a kaleidoscope of iridescent images and colours.

"Like wow," Sara said, her voice dripping with sarcasm, "Square-eyes knows how to activate screen-savers."

"A screen-saver that employs fractal mathematics." He turned the displays back off. "I take it you haven't thought of a story yet?"

She shrugged and gnawed on one of her heavily-bitten nails. "No, but does that matter? If your program's worth its salt then it should be able to make a phone-book sound interesting."

"So?"

"So... just write anything. The events of the last half an hour for example."

"A fair suggestion." He paused and hummed to himself. "Okay, you can make yourself useful by loading some necessary data."

"Me? Oh thankyou, my lord and master. Would you like me to wipe your arse as well?"

"There you go with that kinky stuff again." He returned to his tuneless humming, leaving Sara to shake her head and wonder why she indulged him so shamelessly. Gone was the uncommunicative, hesitant creature she started out with a year ago. Now he could debate with her on nearly every subject. Amazing the difference a women's touch can make!

She accessed the appropriate files, made the required system adjustments then pressed 'reboot'. The work-station made a timid beep that belied the immense processing power of the big Unix system. Sara once joked to a friend that NASA rented her gear to plot their space shots.

There was a second beep and the big hard-drive went quiet. She typed in her password and handed control back to John.

He wasted no time. The word processor sprang to life,

Sara watched the words appear in their final form. The result was less than perfect, but the prose did seem to have more energy. She leaned forward in her seat and said, "You've forgotten something."

"Oh? Like what?" He transcribed her words into the story even as he answered.

"A title, you idiot."

"Ah... easy fixed. And just for good measure I'll write it on the end as well."

He paused and hummed to himself again. Sara liked to think that the sound indicated satisfaction, but inwardly she knew better. Computers - even super-smart ones like John - had a big problem feeling anything at all.

She patted the top of his cabinet with affection as he wrote in the final words, "You taught me everything I know."